9|4

HAYNER PLD/DOWNTOWN
OVERDUES .10 PER DAY. MAXIMUM
FINE COST OF ITEM. LOST OR
DAMAGED ITEM ADDITIONAL $5.00
SERVICE CHARGE
HOMEBOUND

YOU AND I

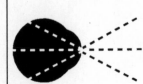

This Large Print Book carries the
Seal of Approval of N.A.V.H.

You and I

Jacquelin Thomas

THORNDIKE PRESS

A part of Gale, Cengage Learning

GALE
CENGAGE Learning

Detroit • New York • San Francisco • New Haven, Conn • Waterville, Maine • London

GALE
CENGAGE Learning

LIBRARY OF CONGRESS CATALOGING-IN-PUBLICATION DATA

Thomas, Jacquelin.
  You and I / by Jacquelin Thomas. — Large print ed.
    p. cm. — (Thorndike Press large print African-American)
  ISBN-13: 978-1-4104-3918-5
  ISBN-10: 1-4104-3918-6
  1. African Americans—Fiction. 2. Large type books. I. Title.
PS3570.H5637Y68 2011
813'.54—dc22   2011015349

Published in 2011 by arrangement with Harlequin Books S.A.

Printed in Mexico
1 2 3 4 5 6 7 15 14 13 12 11

Bernard, you are my best friend
and the love of my life.
There are no words
to adequately express
how honored I am to be your wife.
Thank you for being my
#1 fan and supporter.
Other men should follow your example
as a husband, father and friend.

Dear Reader,

A lot of women feel pressured to lose weight because of the way women are often portrayed in some of pop culture's magazines, movies and television shows. Cherise Ransom has never been thin, but it isn't until she's an adult that she understands the importance of loving herself and being a size healthy.

My inspiration for this story was an article I read about an eleven-year-old who committed suicide after being teased by classmates because he was overweight. This tragedy prompted me to highlight Cherise's struggles as an overweight teen and her desire to fit in with her peers, which leads to a mistake that haunts her many years later as an adult. But will it come between her and the man she falls in love with?

I hope you enjoy *You and I*. I am also looking forward to introducing you to the Alexander family of Beverly Hills in the coming months.

I love hearing from my readers, so please feel free to contact me on the following:

Facebook: www.facebook.com/jacquelin thomas

Twitter: www.twitter.com/jacquelinthomas
Web: www.jacquelinthomas.com
Email: jacquelinthomas@yahoo.com

Blessings to you,
Jacquelin Thomas

CHAPTER 1

"I can't believe you have another brother and that I have another cousin," Cherise Ransom told Elle as they stood in line for the duck with chocolate sauce that everyone at the wedding reception had been raving about.

"I know," Elle murmured. "It's eleven of us now."

"Well, we call ourselves a clan — I guess it's true. Especially with all of the marriages and children — there's a bunch of Ransoms running around Los Angeles." Cherise's gaze traveled once more to where Ransom Winters was standing with his bride, Coco, holding court.

"He's definitely related, though," she said. "He looks just like us. I think it's pretty cool that his mother named him Ransom. I guess she wanted him to have his father's name in some way."

Cherise glanced over her shoulder at a

woman standing nearby and said in a low voice, "Aunt Amanda sure seems to be taking it well."

Elle gave a slight shrug. "He's not hard to love at all. Ransom is a really neat guy, and he was an instant fit with the family. As for my mama, she wants to leave the past behind. Ransom was conceived when she and my dad were separated."

"Sometimes the past definitely has a way of catching up with you," Cherise responded, staring straight ahead, watching the bride and groom, but her mind was somewhere else, in another place and time.

Elle followed her gaze and said, "Ransom and Coco make a beautiful couple, don't you think?"

Cherise nodded, bringing her thoughts back to the present. "I want someone to come knock me off my feet like that."

"The right guy is going to show up when you least expect it, cousin."

She met Elle's smile with one of her own. "I really hope so. You and Brennen are crazy in love, and you've just had another baby. All of you . . . well, all except Ivy, are deliriously happy. To be honest with you, sometimes I get a little sad being around all the love and happiness."

"Now you sound like Ivy," Elle pointed

out with a light chuckle.

"See, that's who I need to start hanging out with," Cherise said. "She and I are on the same page. We can be lonely together."

Elle passed on the chocolate-dusted scallops with vanilla butter sauce, while Cherise decided to give them a try. "Not too much," she told the server. "Thanks."

Cherise made her way back to the table, following Elle. She sat down next to her.

"Girl, there's so much chocolate at this reception, I can feel myself putting on pounds. You know that's the last thing I need right now," Cherise said, picking up one of the elegantly designed boxes of chocolate truffles.

"You need to stop that, Cherise," Elle told her. "You look beautiful."

"She sure does," a man said from behind them.

Cherise turned around in her chair. "Hi, Daddy." She rose to her feet to give her father a hug.

"Uncle Jules, where have you been?" Elle asked. "I tried to call you last week."

"I was in Raleigh, North Carolina. An old friend of mine is terminally ill, and so a bunch of us decided to go up and spend some time with him." He stroked his daughter's shoulder. "I've told you about talk like

11

that, Cherise. And look at your plate. You hardly have anything on it."

"Don't get me wrong, I'm happy with the way I look," she quickly explained. "But I can't just go crazy when it comes to food. I want to be healthy and keep off the extra pounds, so I eat smaller portions. I'm a full-figured gal and proud of it." Cherise sat back down.

Elle hugged her. "I'm so proud of you. I remember when you came to live with us and how much your weight bothered you. You've grown up to be this beautiful and extremely confident woman, and now you're helping other girls do the same."

"I'm just trying to get them to focus on being a size healthy versus a size four." Cherise was proud of her work as a counselor at the Darlene Sheppard Center, a therapeutic community for overweight children and teens.

Her father spent a few more minutes with them before moving on to talk to some of the other guests. Cherise was glad to see him, although he stayed on the go — had always been that way, which is one of the reasons her parents had divorced. The other was that he loved women and hadn't been exactly faithful, but Cherise loved her father in spite of his flaws. Out of all of her siblings, she was the closest to him.

The newlyweds gradually made their way over to where Elle and Cherise were sitting.

"Congratulations," Cherise said. She wiped her mouth on the cloth napkin before continuing. "The ceremony was beautiful."

Ransom gave her a hug. "What's up, cousin? I just met your sister."

"Jazz wasn't sure she was going to make it," Cherise responded. "But she really wanted to meet you. Coco, you look stunning."

"I was about to tell you the same thing," she responded. "Cherise, how are the girls?"

Coco was referring to the teenagers Cherise counseled at the center. She had taken them on a tour of the Stanley Chocolates factory, which was owned by Coco's family, and for drinking chocolate at the Chocolate Bar next door, owned by Coco.

"They have their challenges," she answered. "But I'm trying to work with them."

"Cherise, when Coco and I get back, I'd like to talk to you about working with the structured day program," Ransom said. "I've wanted to get something started for girls."

She nodded. "We'll definitely talk when you get back."

When they walked away, Elle turned to

Cherise and asked, "So are you going on the family cruise with us next month? We're going to the Mediterranean this year."

"You guys are all coupled off," Cherise responded. "I tried to get Jazz to go with me, but she's not going to be able to, so I think I'm going to sit this one out. Besides, the ship is probably full by now."

"Ivy's going," Elle said. "She booked a family suite because we thought more were coming, but some people had to back out."

Cherise shook her head. "I think I'm going to just wait for the next one. I'm not prepared to go on a cruise this year."

"Please come on the cruise so that I'll have somebody to hang out with, Cherise," Ivy Ransom, one of Elle's sisters, said as she joined them. "It's just me and the girls in a huge suite. You can stay with us."

She was still undecided. Cherise enjoyed being with her cousins, but she often felt like the odd man out, because most of them were married or involved in a committed relationship. Her brother Julian was going on the cruise and taking some girl he'd recently started dating. Ivy was divorced and bitter — Cherise didn't want to hear her complaining the entire trip. If she decided to go, she wanted to have fun.

"I have to think about this for a moment,"

Cherise said.

"Well, I've already paid for someone and she's not going to be able to go, so just let me know if you can go in her place. I'll call the cruise line to change the information." Ivy sat down at the table with them. She glanced over her shoulder at the man sitting beside her mother and said, "I still can't believe Mama brought a date to the wedding. First she brings him to the Valentine's Day dinner and now he's showing up for the family dinners on Sunday. What exactly is going on between her and Mr. Ragland?"

"Mama told me that they were just friends," Elle said. "I know that he's a prominent attorney and seems to be a nice man. He lost his wife a few years back."

"I don't want him hurting Mom," Ivy snapped.

"I don't think there's anything to worry about," Elle responded. "Mr. Ragland seems to be quite infatuated with Mama. Look at him — he can't keep his eyes off her."

"Even Aunt Amanda can get a man — I know I need to step up my game," Cherise said with a chuckle.

"Mama's still sexy," Elle said, laughing softly. "Don't be fooled by that cane. She's still got her groove."

"Oh, Lord," Ivy muttered, shaking her

head. "Please tell me that our oh-so-Christian mother is not sleeping with Mr. Ragland."

Cherise hid her smile behind her napkin at the horrified expression on Ivy's face. She could be such a prude sometimes.

"I don't think she is, but since I don't live at home anymore I don't really know for sure. But Ivy . . . even if she is — she's a grown woman," Elle told her sister.

Ivy stood up with purpose. "I'm going to have a talk with her."

"Do it at your own risk," Elle warned. "I'm going to stay over here and just mind my own business."

"Me, too," Cherise intoned.

Her uncle had died a long time ago, so Cherise was glad to see her aunt Amanda enjoying the company of a man.

Ivy sat back down. "Mom can take care of herself, I suppose. But back to you, Cherise. I really hope you'll come on the cruise. I don't want to be the only single person in the clan."

Cherise excused herself to make a visit to the ladies' room, where she eyed her reflection. She was five nine and full-figured — no doubt about that. Her flawless mahogany complexion was devoid of heavy makeup, and her dark brown hair fell past her shoulders in waves. She wasn't bad-looking. She just wasn't one of those thin types that a lot of men seemed to love.

Cherise thought about her options. She believed her Mr. Right was somewhere close — maybe he'd be aboard the *Emerald Princess*. That's how her cousin Laine had met his wife. But even if he wasn't, looking was part of the fun, she decided as she thought about the scores of men that would be on the ship.

When she returned to the table, Cherise announced, "Okay, I've made a decision."

"This is their existing facility," Steven Chambers began as he pointed to a photograph on the board. "There's about thirteen thousand square feet of space. They're entering into a major facility expansion of about forty thousand square feet of building space on the new site. I'm going in this afternoon to present the new design to the church executive board to get their feedback."

His supervisor nodded in approval. "The pastor of this church is a good friend of mine. It's important that we know exactly what he wants to achieve in this project."

"I started doing a schematic design after I spoke with Pastor Wilkins last week," Steven said, "but before I finish it, I need more information."

"Wilkins was very impressed with the new Holton Building, and he insisted on having you as the lead on this project."

Steven straightened his tie and smiled. "Thanks, Randall. After my meeting this afternoon, I'm off for the next fourteen days. I'm really looking forward to this vacation."

"Enjoy," Randall said. "You've earned it."

Steven left his supervisor's office and took the stairs down to the parking garage situated in downtown Los Angeles. He entered the freeway and headed toward Inglewood to meet with Pastor Wilkins and his staff.

In a few days he would be aboard the *Emerald Princess,* cruising toward the Mediterranean. The last time he went on vacation was with his ex-girlfriend. It had been almost six months since that relationship ended. He had cared deeply for the woman but knew that they had no future, especially since she already had a husband in northern California. Steven had had no idea that he was involved with a married woman until her husband confronted him.

His cell phone rang, the custom ring tone letting him know that it was his favorite aunt — his other mom — who was calling.

Steven grinned as he clicked on the speakerphone. "Aunt Eula Mae, how's life in Ghana?" She and her husband had been living there for the past ten years because of his work.

"It's still beautiful here," she responded. "But I'm ready to come back to the States. I miss y'all so much."

"Mama and I were just talking about you yesterday," he said. "We miss you too. I thought Uncle Jerome was planning to retire this year."

She released a long sigh. "I thought so too, but I guess we both were wrong. Jerome wants to stay here for another year. That man is tapping on my last nerve with this job of his. I've told him that I'm leaving him."

Steven laughed. "Aunt Eula Mae, you're not going anywhere."

"I'm ready to come back to the States. Hey, you haven't gotten married on me yet, have you?"

He laughed. "You know I haven't. I can't get married until you meet her. I don't know what it is about you and Mom, but you can definitely spot toxic women." They had both warned him about all the ones he dated and, as it turned out, they'd been right on the money. Steven trusted his aunt and mom because they had been wonderful role models for him, and he respected their opinions.

Steven chatted with his aunt for most of the drive home.

"I'm here at the church, Aunt Eula Mae. I'll give you a call back before I leave for Barcelona tonight. I'm flying there a few days early so that I can spend some time in Spain before the cruise."

"Have fun, hon."

He smiled. "I intend to do just that."

Steven disconnected the call and shut off the car.

Humming softly, he got out of the car and headed inside the church. Once the presentation was over, Steven planned to stop home long enough to change into something comfortable and grab his luggage and passport, then drive to the airport. He was looking forward to this cruise.

"Well, look at you, Cherise," Elle said when they were in Bloomingdale's at the Beverly Center. "And you were worried about wearing a swimsuit. Girl, you look good."

"Elle, are you sure?" Cherise peered into the mirror, staring critically at her curvy size fourteen torso, and even she had to admit the black one-piece swimsuit with ruching and well-placed ruffles flattered her full figure. "I guess it doesn't look bad."

She smiled over the fact that she looked younger than her twenty-five years. "No, not bad at all. So, are you ready to wow everyone on the cruise ship and the Mediterranean, cousin?"

Elle picked up a neon-green swimsuit and responded, "Not quite. I like this one, but it's a little too bright for me."

Cherise stole one last glimpse at the mirror. "Okay, I'm getting this one."

When she walked out of the dressing room, Cherise and Elle strolled up to the counter and paid for the items Cherise had selected for the cruise. They left the boutique and walked down the street to a nearby restaurant for lunch.

"I don't know why I waited until the last minute to shop for the cruise. When did I decide to go?"

"At Ransom and Coco's reception," Elle responded with a smile. "That was almost a month ago, but you have always been a procrastinator when it comes to stuff like this."

"Now, two days before the cruise, I'm running around like I'm crazy," Cherise said with a chuckle. "I'm really looking forward to this vacation. I don't know why, but I have a feeling that something good is going to happen."

Early on the tenth of July, the large Ransom family boarded a plane to Barcelona, Spain. The clan was broken into smaller groups for the flight over. Laine and Ray and their families had left the night before. Garrett and his family wanted to spend some time in Barcelona, so they'd traveled to Spain a week earlier.

Ivy and Cherise and her brother were on the same flight, while Elle, Jillian and some of the others were on another one with a different airline. They would be arriving within an hour of each other.

Cherise could've kissed the ground when she walked off the plane. It had taken nineteen hours, which included two layovers, but they were finally in Barcelona.

"I'm so glad to get off that plane," Ivy said, stretching. She glanced down at her daughters, who were yawning and stretching too. "My babies did so well during the flight. I'm so proud of them."

"Me, too," Cherise responded. "I like flying, but I'm discovering that I'm not crazy about long flights."

"I'ma walk down here to see if Sherrie made it in yet," her brother said.

"Julian, why didn't she fly with us?" Cherise asked.

"She works for U.S. Air," he responded. "I had already made my reservations before I met Sherrie."

Ivy and Cherise sat down with Ivy's daughters to grab a bite to eat while they waited for the plane carrying Elle, Jillian and the others to come in.

"We're going to have a great time on the cruise," Cherise told Ivy, who suddenly looked sad.

"The last time we went on one, Charles was with me."

Cherise reached over and gave Ivy's hand a light squeeze. "It's his loss."

She smiled and nodded.

The girls were getting restless and fretful, so Cherise and Ivy attempted to keep them busy until the others arrived. They both sighed with relief when the other plane arrived on time.

After everyone had arrived and were gathered together, they made their way through customs and baggage claim. Outside the terminal, two stretch limos were waiting to whisk them off to the hotel where they would meet up with the rest of the family.

It was around four when they finally

reached the hotel. Some family members wanted to do some sightseeing, but Cherise opted to go straight to her room and sleep until it was time for dinner. She didn't like sleeping on planes, so she could barely keep her eyes open.

Cherise was asleep by the time her head touched the pillow.

She didn't get up until shortly after seven, when she showered, slipped on a sundress, then rushed off to meet her relatives downstairs.

Laine had prearranged for them to eat in one of the private dining rooms at El Gran Café, since there were almost forty people in their group. They were once again transported by stretch limousines.

The large dining room had lovely hardwood floors and enormous windows adorned with rich, red velvet curtains. Laine and his wife, Regis, had preselected the menu of seafood croquettes and prawns with garlic for starters, followed by a choice of roasted lamb, monkfish or a veal fillet with foie gras and mushroom sauce, and for dessert, caramelized crema catalana, a specialty of the restaurant.

Afterward, everyone retired to their hotel rooms to settle in for the evening.

Cherise and Ivy weren't tired and decided

to watch a movie together in Ivy's room.

While her daughters slept, Ivy said, "I'm not sure I can do this."

"Do what?"

"Raise them by myself," she responded. "Cherise, it's hard, and I'm so tired all the time. I'm taking on more shifts now at the hospital, since I can't depend on Charles to do what he's supposed to do."

Ivy was a registered nurse, and until her separation and divorce had worked two days a week.

"You are going to go after him for child support, right?" Cherise asked.

"He doesn't want to do it through the courts, but I'm going to have to get them involved because now that he's married again, he wants me to be understanding of his financial obligations."

Cherise shook her head. "His new wife and kids don't have anything to do with you. Ivy, you do what you have to do for those girls. As for raising them — you've been the one doing that all along. Charles wasn't always around."

"You're right," Ivy admitted. "He was too busy chasing skirts." She shook her head sadly. "I just wish . . ."

"What?" Cherise asked.

"It doesn't matter," Ivy responded with a

25

dismissive wave of her hand. "There really isn't any need to talk about it. He's a jerk."

Her cell phone rang.

Ivy looked down at it and said, "It's the jerk calling right now."

Cherise wanted to give Ivy some privacy, so she went to her bedroom and placed a quick call to her mother. "I just wanted to let you know that we made it to Spain."

"Julian called me earlier, but we lost our connection," she told Cherise.

"He's been having trouble with his phone since we arrived."

"Jazz really wanted to go, but she just didn't have the money after getting her car repaired and buying that new house."

Cherise was surprised by her mother's words. "Mama, why didn't she come to me? I could've worked something out with her."

"You know your sister. She doesn't like people in her business. Don't you mention that I told you, Cherise, okay? Jazz would be mad."

"I won't say anything." Cherise knew a thing or two about keeping secrets. She had been keeping one for years.

CHAPTER 2

After their stay in Barcelona, the family was transported to the cruise ship. Cherise and Ivy were in the Sapphire Suite on deck nine, which featured two bedrooms, a living area with sofa, dining room and entertainment center, and two bathrooms.

"That suite that Laine and Ray are sharing is nice," Cherise said.

"Carrie told me that they had to have at least eight staying in there to book the suite. It can hold fourteen people. She and Ray have the three kids, and then Laine and Regis have their two, so that's nine. Garrette's kids are staying in there, too, so they almost have fourteen."

Elle and her family were in the owner's suite, while Jillian and Kaitlin and their families shared the Ruby family suite, which featured a loft. The other family members were in staterooms along the ninth and tenth floors.

"I don't know why I agreed to come on this cruise this year," Ivy complained as they waited for the elevator. "You should have talked me out of it. The last thing I want is to be around a bunch of lovers."

"This is what you need, what we both need," Cherise assured Ivy. The doors to the elevator opened and she was struck speechless by the sight of the handsome, dark-skinned brother inside. He smiled, then stepped out of the way to let them enter.

They took the elevator to deck nine.

Cherise noted that he got off on the same floor, following behind them.

When they arrived at the suite, Cherise waited until they were inside before asking, "Did you happen to get a good look at that fine hunk on the elevator with us? He got off on this floor."

Ivy shrugged nonchalantly. "He looked like any other man."

Cherise's eyes opened wide in response to her cousin's comment. "Ivy, have you gone blind? That man was gorgeous."

"Well, he just didn't look that hot to me, that's all."

"If you say so . . ." Cherise muttered, almost to herself.

Inside their suite, Ivy turned to Cherise

and said, "It's not that I hate men or anything like that. I'm just not in the mood for games or trying to figure out if I'm being played. I have two small daughters to worry about, and I have to protect them. They are my first priority."

Cherise nodded in understanding. "I know Charles didn't do right by you, but just don't forget that there are still some nice men out there, Ivy."

Ivy pulled a stack of clothes from the suitcase and placed them in a drawer. "I actually had a nice guy a long time ago, but I was foolish. I dumped him to be with Charles. I've learned that everything that glitters ain't gold. That's for sure."

"You're talking about Michael Stanley?" Cherise asked from the doorway. "Coco's brother? I remember when you two were dating."

Ivy nodded. "He's a sweetheart. Back then, nice guys seemed so boring."

Cherise went to her room and put away her clothing. When she finished, she walked into Ivy's room, asking, "Have you looked at our itinerary yet?"

"We're at sea all day tomorrow, and on Friday we'll be in Malta," Ivy responded. "On Saturday we go to Tunisia, and then on to Naples. I really want to see the ruins of Pompeii."

"I promised Jazz I'd get lots of pictures for her," Cherise said as she helped Ivy put away the children's clothing. "I wish that she could've come with us."

Ivy wanted to lie down with her daughters, so Cherise decided to check on her brother. She walked out of her suite and bumped into something muscular and solid.

"I'm so sorry," she murmured, looking up. Cherise straightened and tried to act normal when she recognized that the fine piece of chocolate standing outside her suite was the man from the elevator.

"No problem." He flashed a big smile that warmed her all over.

Their eyes met and held.

He's fine . . . ooh this man is so fine . . . those big strong arms and his lips . . .

Cherise pushed away her lustful thoughts lest she actually verbalize what she was thinking. She cleared her throat awkwardly.

"My name is Steven Chambers," he told her, holding out his hand. "It looks like we're going to be neighbors for the next ten days."

Grinning, she shook his hand. "I'm Cherise Ransom. It's really nice to meet you, Steven."

"I'm in the room right there," he said,

pointing.

God was really testing her by putting this man right across from her room. If Ivy and the children weren't in the suite with her . . .

Cherise burst into a short laugh, then said, "I'm sorry. I think I'm a little giddy from jet lag." She wasn't about to tell him what she'd really been thinking about.

"It's fine. I love to laugh myself."

"Well, I guess I'll be seeing you around," Cherise said, then groaned inwardly. She hoped she didn't sound like she was coming on to him.

"I hope so," Steven responded. He gave her one last look of admiration before walking away.

This cruise was off to a great start, she decided with a grin.

He loved the sound of her laughter.

So far, so good, Steven thought to himself as he watched Cherise walk down the hallway away from the suites. He'd noticed her earlier on the elevator with another woman, and wondered if she was sailing with a friend or relative.

He had noticed that she wore no wedding ring on her left hand, but after what happened before, he wasn't just going to assume she was single. However, Steven intended to find out the next chance he got. One thing for certain, he would be sure to run into Cherise on several occasions over the next ten days.

He had debated whether or not to take a cruise this year and was glad that he'd decided to do it. He had enjoyed his time in Barcelona, taking in the rich tapestry of the city where the past blended with the future. He found La Sagrada Família, the most ambitious work of Barcelona's Antoni Gaudí, truly awe-inspiring. Steven had also visited Jean Nouvel's luminous Torre Agbar, which was considered the most daring addition to Barcelona's skyline since the first towers of La Sagrada Família went up.

Steven returned to his suite after a short stroll to locate the basketball court and the gym. He stifled a yawn and considered lying down for an hour before going down to the pool for a swim, but then remembered the emergency drill they were required to attend.

Steven picked up the novel he'd brought along with him and settled down on the sofa to read until it was time for the drill.

His mind drifted back to Cherise. He really wanted to have another conversation with her. Steven couldn't put his finger on it, but there was something special about her.

"You look great, Cherise, so stop worrying," Elle said, leaning against the rail. "C'mon, everyone is waiting for us at the pool."

"Where is the baby?"

"With Daisi," Elle responded, referring to her sister-in-law. "She can't swim, so she said she'd watch Briana. Kaitlin's going to take Chandler to her as well."

As they stepped outside, Cherise beheld her surroundings. It was so amazing the way the sun seemed to wash the ocean in brilliant waves of color.

"Cherise, we haven't been out here more than five minutes and you're already getting stares from all of the men out here."

Laughing, she shook her head. "You're crazy, Elle. You know you're the one they're looking at."

"I think it's you." She stopped walking. "Oh my goodness, I don't believe it."

Shading her eyes, Cherise followed Elle's gaze. Standing nearby was a tall, slender man with a clean-shaven head and dark skin that seemed to glisten in the July sun. Even on his slim frame, muscles bulged everywhere. His swim trunks hung low on his hips. The effect was so devastating — so

33

sexual. It didn't seem fair. There wasn't an ounce of fat on Steven's body, and muscles rippled in all the right places. Her skin began to tingle.

"You know him?"

"Yeah. He did some architecture work for Brennen," Elle responded. "I've only been around Steven a couple of times, but he seems really nice."

"Elle, he's the guy I was just telling you about," Cherise told her. "The one I met in the hallway. His suite is across from mine."

"He's the sexy guy you were talking about? It's a small world." Grinning from ear to ear, Elle waved. "I guess he is nice-looking. I never really noticed before."

Steven waved back.

Cherise ran her fingers through her hair. The thought of seeing Steven again made her nervous. "Well, you're married to Brennen Cunningham — it's probably hard to see beyond that man. He's not exactly hard on the eyes."

Elle cut her eyes at Cherise. "Have you been eyeing my man?"

"Only when you weren't looking," Cherise responded with a chuckle.

"Hello, ladies." Steven's deep, sexy voice greeted them as they walked up to him.

Elle reached up and hugged him. "I can't

believe you're here. Talk about a small world. I was just telling my cousin that you and Brennen have worked together in the past."

Never taking his eyes off of Cherise, he murmured, "It *is* a small world. Is Brennen here with you?"

"He should be down here shortly," Elle responded. "Steven, would you like to join us? We're going to spend some time around the pool. Oh, I'm sorry. You might be with someone."

Cherise held her breath awaiting his response. She hadn't seen him with anyone, but that didn't mean he was vacationing alone.

Steven dropped down to sit beside Elle. "I'm here by my lonesome, I'm afraid."

Elle nodded. "Well, how have you been?"

"Busy working." He turned to face Cherise. "What about you, Cherise? Are you traveling with someone?"

Cherise shook her head. "Nope. Outside of my family here on the ship, I'm solo."

He had the prettiest brown eyes she'd ever seen. They were a mixture of various shades of earth-born colors that had been warmed by the sun. Those gorgeous eyes were now gazing at her left hand.

"You're not married, then?"

Cherise smiled. "No, I don't have a husband." She hoped he couldn't hear the regret in her voice.

"I'm glad to hear that."

Raising an eyebrow, Cherise asked, "Really?"

Elle removed her sarong. "Well, on that note, I think I'll go for a swim. You two just stay here and chat." She winked at Cherise. "Have fun."

Wearing a swimsuit that featured bold lime-green flowers against a black background, Elle sashayed to the water's edge.

"I'm afraid my cousin's not very subtle," Cherise said.

"Neither am I." Steven's dark brown eyes met hers. "The truth is that I was hoping to run into you again."

"Really? Why is that?"

Steven inclined his head. "Cherise, I find you very beautiful and I'm intrigued. I want to know more about you."

Cherise scanned his face to discern if he was running game, but he seemed sincere. She relaxed a bit.

Steven found a couple of empty lounge chairs for them to sit down and continue their conversation.

Members of Cherise's family began drifting down to the pool area.

Brennen came and sat down beside Steven. While the two men talked, Cherise was joined by Ivy, who sat down on her other side. "You work fast," Ivy whispered.

"Who's the hunk?" Jillian asked, dropping down beside Ivy. They all spoke in hushed tones.

Ivy glanced at her sister. "Are you serious? He ain't all that."

"I guess you need glasses then," Jillian retorted. "That man over there is fine."

Laughing, Cherise agreed.

Jillian's husband walked up and grabbed her by the hand. "Let's test out the water."

They left.

"You have a huge family," Steven said, when Ivy disappeared with her daughters in tow.

"You have no idea. The others haven't come down yet," Cherise responded with a chuckle. "It's a bunch of us."

His eyes widened in surprise. "It's a family reunion?"

She nodded. "In a way. It's just mostly the siblings and cousins that go on the cruise. We leave the elders at home, but then they go on their own cruise as well. This year, they are sailing to Mexico in October."

"That's pretty cool," he said.

"Elle has five — no — six brothers and

four sisters. I have three brothers and one sister. She and Julian, my brother that's here on the ship, are twins. He's the only one who came this time."

"Wow," Steven murmured. "I always wanted siblings. I'm an only child."

Cherise smiled. "There were times when I wanted to be the only child in the family."

He laughed. "Well, it looks like you all are pretty close."

"We are," Cherise confirmed.

"Steven, why don't you join us?" Brennen asked, when he climbed out of the pool. "We have dinner reservations at Torino's."

"I'd love to," he answered.

Cherise rose to her feet. "I think I'm going to check out this pool. How about you?"

Steven shaded his eyes with his hand. "Is that an invitation?"

"Sure," she responded.

Elle and Jillian watched in amusement as Cherise strolled toward them with Steven. They paused at the pool and Cherise stepped in, wading toward the middle.

He did a surface dive and sank into the water near her.

Cherise felt the water shift as he dove in. She pushed wet hair out of her eyes and moved away as he playfully splashed water in her direction.

"Two can play at this game, mister." She burst into laughter.

After frolicking in the water with Cherise as if they were children, Steven climbed out to get something for them to drink.

"Looks like the two of you are getting along well," Elle whispered in Cherise's ear.

"We are," she whispered back.

Elle pulled herself out of the water. "I'm going up to check on Briana and take a nap. I'll see you all at dinner."

"Your cousin's leaving?" Steven asked.

She nodded. "She wants to go check on her baby."

Cherise splashed water on Steven and swam away.

"Oh, you want to play games, huh?" Steven raced behind her. "Wait until I catch up with you . . ."

He left the threat floating on the wind.

Steven smiled to himself as he watched Cherise frolicking in the pool with her cousins. He still couldn't get over how many Ransoms were on the ship. He liked that they were all so close.

As mesmerizing as the ocean surrounding them was, Steven couldn't take his eyes off of her. He thought of her smooth, deep mahogany complexion, big brown eyes and the way her long hair waved up when wet. She was an extremely beautiful woman. Not thin but not too heavy either, curvy and thick. Just the right size.

Tapping him on the shoulder, Cherise asked, "What are you thinking about so hard?"

Steven snapped out of his reverie. Standing waist deep in the water, he confessed, "I was thinking about you, actually."

"You just don't quit, do you?" Laughing, she playfully splashed water at him.

"I'm serious."

Cherise shook her head. "Let's not get serious about anything. We're on vacation — let's enjoy this time together. We should be having fun."

Steven thought Cherise looked almost sad when she'd said that, but the expression quickly dissipated. He told himself that it was only his imagination.

CHAPTER 3

Cherise took digital photos of historic St. John's Cathedral in Valletta, Malta, stepping gently over the engraved marble tombstones covering the cathedral's floor, marking the final resting places of knights.

Steven was following behind her, taking pictures with his camera. Every now and then, he would open a sketchbook and start drawing with intensity, absorbed by his vision.

He was clearly an art lover. Cherise soon discovered that they both shared a love for art history. They toured the Grand Master's Palace, which served as the office of the president and the seat of the Maltese Parliament.

"Are you interested in seeing the Auberge de Castille?" Steven asked Cherise. "I read that it's one of the finest architectural works here in Malta."

"Sure, I'd like to check it out," she responded. "You're an architect, so you definitely can't leave Malta without seeing it."

"According to the guide, the building houses the office of the Prime Minister."

Steven pulled Cherise closer to him as they neared a group of seedy-looking guys standing near an alley. He didn't release her until they were back with other passengers from the ship.

When he placed his muscled arms around her, Cherise could only define it as feeling as if she'd come home. She felt safe with him.

Cherise received a text from Elle and said, "My cousins have had enough of history. They are going to Ta'Qali Handicrafts Village. They want to see the glass-blowing factory."

"You're sure you wouldn't rather go with them?" Steven asked.

Cherise planted her hands on her hips. "Are you implying that since I'm a woman, I want to spend my day shopping?"

He laughed and held up his hands in defense of an attack. "Not at all. I just know that you're on a family vacation, and I don't want to keep you from spending time with them."

"No, we're going to the Auberge de

Castille," Cherise stated in a tone that brooked no argument. "They're planning to spend the rest of afternoon soaking up the sun on the beach. I'll meet them then." She was enjoying her time with Steven. She could see her family anytime.

After touring the Auberge de Castille, they visited a nearby art gallery.

Cherise and Steven grabbed a bite to eat. After they finished, they strolled along the cobblestone streets toward the port.

"Malta is absolutely beautiful," Cherise murmured. "The buildings here are nothing like I've seen before."

Steven agreed as he finished off his drink. "This is more of an Arabic architecture. You need more than one day to really explore the city. I wish I could see more of the architectural design."

"I think I'd like to come back here one day, but not on a cruise." Cherise checked her watch. "I guess I need to head down to the beach for some family time. What are you getting ready to do?" She silently hoped that he would be willing to join her.

"I don't have any plans," Steven responded. "If I'm not imposing, I'd like to spend the rest of my day with you."

She grinned. "I'm so glad you said that. Did you bring a swimsuit?"

He nodded. "I have one in my backpack. I'm always prepared."

Cherise warmed beneath his gaze. Steven seemed almost too perfect, but then she had only known him for a couple of days. She knew that he lived in Los Angeles, too, and wondered briefly if they would stay in touch once they got home. She hoped so.

Cherise tried not to let the rivulets of water streaming down Steven's face to his hairy chest distract her from all the beauty around her. He was a very sexy man indeed, she had to admit. When he caught her staring at him, he grinned knowingly.

Clearing her throat, she turned away.

"It looks like you two are really clicking," Elle whispered in her ear.

"We're enjoying ourselves, but I have no expectations beyond this cruise. We have a good time together, but it's not like he wants a relationship."

"Are you open to it, if he does?" Elle asked.

Cherise smiled. "I'll take it day by day."

Elle swam over to her husband while Cherise sought out Steven.

They got out of the water and sat down on towels.

Cherise and Steven talked about the new

project he was working on and her desire to land the position as a senior counselor at the center.

"Watching you with your little cousins, I can tell you're good with young people," Steven said. "I think what you're doing is great, Cherise."

"I know from experience what they're going through, so it's easy for me to relate." She picked up a handful of sand, relishing the grainy texture as it slid through her fingers.

Elle and Brennen walked out of the water dripping wet, and joined them twenty minutes later.

"So what did you buy when you guys went shopping earlier?" Cherise asked Elle.

"Believe it or not, I didn't get a thing. Jillian picked up some stuff though. She left one boutique with two bags of shoes."

An hour later, Steven stretched and yawned. "I'm tired, so I think I'm going to head on back to the boat and take a nap." Brushing sand off of his swim trunks, he added, "I'll see y'all later tonight."

Cherise stood up to give Steven a hug. "I'll see you later."

"I'd be careful if I were you," Ivy muttered as she straightened her hat. "You and Steven have been spending a lot of time together."

"He's a nice guy, Ivy," Elle interjected. "Let Cherise enjoy herself. You should be doing the same thing. That guy Montel has been trying to get your attention from the moment we stepped on the ship."

"Hmph," Ivy uttered. "He can keep right on trying, but I'm not interested."

Picking up her tote, Cherise said, "Ivy, I'm just having fun with a handsome man. I don't have any illusions about anything. I'm here to have a good time on my vacation. You should try it."

Ivy groaned and walked away, shaking her head.

Elle and Cherise laughed.

It was time for them to head back to the boat, so they gathered up towels, totes and children.

Inside the ship, Cherise followed Ivy into the suite. She sank down on the edge of the king-size bed. "I am so tired."

Ivy dropped down beside her. "Cherise, I'm really glad you and Steven are spending time together. He seems like a real nice guy. I just say the things I do so that I can keep my family from trying to set me up with a guy."

"Steven and I have a good time together and I enjoy his company." Cherise strolled into the bathroom and jumped into the shower.

Afterward, she climbed into bed and fell asleep as soon as her head hit the fluffy pillow. Cherise slept until Ivy woke her up an hour later. She and the girls were already dressed for dinner.

Later, Ivy stuck the last hairpin in Cherise's upswept hairstyle. "You look gorgeous," she told Cherise. "When Steven sees you tonight, I'm not sure you'll be able to get rid of the man."

Laughing, Cherise turned away from the mirror to face Ivy. "I don't know about all that." Deep down, she hoped her cousin was right, but she didn't want to get her hopes up.

"Just wait until he sees you."

Cherise stood up and took off her robe. Reaching for the magenta dress she was going to wear to dinner, she added, "Ivy, I have a confession to make. The truth is that I really like him. Steven and I seem to really click. I can't explain it, but we have so much in common."

"Steven seems like one heck of a catch," Ivy said. "And from what I've heard about him, it sounds like he's definitely husband material."

As she zipped up her dress, Cherise broke

into a smile. "You need to follow your own advice, Ivy. Have you even said more than two words to Montel?"

"I'm not interested in him. There is only one man I'd like to spend time with right now and he's not on this boat." Ivy headed to the mirror to inspect her appearance. "Montel is nice, but he comes with a lot of drama."

Cherise folded her arms across her chest and asked, "So what's up with him?" She watched Ivy apply her makeup like a pro.

Without missing a beat, she replied, "Oh, he has seven children by five different women for starters."

Ivy applied her lipstick, and her look was completed.

"Oh, yeah, that's straight crazy," Cherise said. "You definitely don't need that. As for Steven, I'm just going to see what happens, Ivy. I'm taking it one day at a time." Cherise powdered her face and applied a clear gloss to her lips.

She stole a peek at the clock. It was almost time to head downstairs.

Some of their relatives were waiting in the lobby when they stepped off the elevator. Cherise spotted Steven among them.

"You ladies look beautiful," he said.

"Thank you," Ivy and Cherise chorused.

Steven placed Cherise's hand on his arm and led her into the dining room. Speaking low enough for her ears only, he said, "Cherise, you are truly a sight. Your dress looks like it was inspired by the South Seas."

Cherise smiled. "Thank you," she murmured softly. She had never met a man who was able to find beauty in almost everything. *Even me,* she mused silently, and the thought pleased her immensely.

Cherise woke up early and headed straight to the gym. She was surprised to see Steven already there working out.

"I didn't know you'd be here this morning," she told him.

"This is how I usually start my day," Steven responded. "I figured I'd do the same while on vacation."

She nodded in agreement. This was something else they had in common. Cherise made a point of going to the gym at least three times a week.

Cherise got on the treadmill beside him. "Don't be offended, but I don't usually talk when I'm working out."

Steven smiled, then stuck a set of earphones in his ears.

She did the same.

Once Cherise was in her zone, Steven

49

ceased to exist while she focused on her workout. She was determined to maintain her weight while on the cruise, although all the wonderful food didn't make it easy.

The ship was slowing down as it pulled into port. They had arrived in Tunis, Tunisia. Cherise finished her workout and then went through a series of stretching exercises.

Steven joined her as she was finishing up.

On the way back to their suites, Steven said, "Brennen invited me to join you all today. I hope you don't mind. I don't want you to think that I'm trying to monopolize your time."

Cherise smiled. "No, it's fine, Steven. I enjoy your company and would've asked you myself."

They made plans to meet in thirty minutes.

Ivy had just walked out of her bedroom when Cherise entered the suite. "We need to make sure we dress modestly to respect the traditions of this country," she told her.

Cherise nodded. "There's so much history here in Tunisia. I know we're not going to be able see everything, but I definitely want to visit the ruins of Carthage."

After a quick shower, Cherise selected a modest maxi dress with a thin shawl to drape around her head and shoulders. She slipped on a comfortable pair of sandals and stuck a pair of sneakers into her oversized tote.

They met everyone in the lobby area of the ship.

Cherise couldn't stop smiling when she spotted Steven. Cherise knew the truth. She was falling in love with Steven.

The passengers traveled from the ship via coach to the Tunis city center, but Steven's first glimpse of Tunisia was one of sun-kissed beaches and deep blue seas. It was paradise.

As they strolled the streets of Ville Nouvelle, Steven found himself sketching pictures of Cherise surrounded by French architecture, sidewalk cafés and patisseries.

They wandered through the colorful medina and souks, savoring the sights, sounds and smells enveloping them. He found that Cherise wasn't afraid to try new cultural delicacies and was an avid explorer, preferring to take in the historic attractions instead of shopping.

"What are you drawing now?" she asked, walking over to where he was sitting.

He showed her his artwork.

"Is this really how you see me?" Cherise wanted to know.

"It is."

She smiled. "You're very talented, Steven, and you have an incredible eye for beauty. I'm sure that pastor is going to love the ideas you have for the new church. I also like what you came up with for the new shopping center."

All of a sudden he reached over, pulling her into his arms and out of the street. A man on a bicycle came to a crashing halt, falling. Steven went over to check on him.

If he hadn't pulled her out of the way, the man would've hit her. Cherise could tell that something was wrong with the back wheel of the bicycle. When Steven walked over to her, she inquired, "Is he okay?"

"He's got some cuts and scrapes, but he'll be okay. How about you? I didn't mean to just grab you like that."

"It's fine," she told him.

Her smile always made his heart perform a tiny flip. Steven found himself losing control of his emotions bit by bit. He wasn't able to put a name to what he was feeling, but it was something he hadn't experienced before in his life.

After four hours of sightseeing, Cherise and Steven returned to the boat to rest up before meeting the others for dinner.

Cherise and Ivy settled down in the living room to talk.

"I'm so glad I came on this cruise," she stated.

Ivy smiled. "Me, too. I'm actually having a good time, even though you abandoned me for Steven."

Cherise laughed. "I'm sorry."

"It's fine," Ivy responded with a slight wave of her hand. "The girls and I have spent some quality time as a family."

"Have you heard any more from Charles?"

"He sent me an email. He's upset because I didn't tell him that we were going on a cruise." Her mouth turned downward. "Like I need to clear my schedule with him."

"What did you tell him?"

"That I can take my daughters wherever I want. He needs to pay child support and actually visit the children if he wants to be a part of their lives."

Cherise checked her watch. "I guess we need to get ready for dinner."

Ivy agreed. "I'll go wake the girls."

An hour later, they left the suite. Steven was standing outside their room when they walked out.

"Did you get any rest?" he inquired.

Cherise shook her head. "Ivy and I spent some time together just talking."

He took her by the hand, leading her down the stairs.

Members of her family were already seated when they arrived. She sat down beside her brother. "I haven't seen much of you and Sherrie," Cherise chided.

Julian broke into a grin. "We've been keeping to ourselves."

She felt the heat of Steven's gaze on her and turned her attention to him. He winked at her.

After dinner, Cherise, Steven, Brennen and Elle decided to go dancing.

Walking back to their table, Cherise fanned herself with her hands. "Steven, would you like to take a walk outside? I need to get some air."

"Sure." Steven grabbed her gently by the elbow and led her toward the exit doors.

They strolled outside and he took her by the hand.

Cherise closed her eyes, savoring the feel of the night air on her face.

Steven leaned over and whispered, "I'm really enjoying spending time like this with you, Cherise." He wrapped his arm around her waist.

She glanced up at him. "I am too, Steven." Cherise felt the heat of desire wash over her like waves.

Turning her to face him, Steven leaned over and kissed her softly on the lips. "I've been wanting to do that all night."

In response, Cherise pulled his head down to hers. Their lips met and she felt buffeted by the winds of a savage harmony. Her senses reeled as if short-circuited.

Breaking their kiss, Cherise buried her face against his throat; her trembling limbs clung to him helplessly. She was extremely conscious of where Steven's warm flesh touched her.

"Why are you so quiet?" he asked after a moment.

"I'm thinking that we just shared a great kiss, and as much as I'd like to do it again, I think that maybe we should head back inside. Elle's probably looking for us."

"I love your honesty, Cherise. As for Elle, I don't think she's worried, because she knows that we're together and that I won't let anything happen to you."

"You and Steven have been gone for a quite some time . . ." Elle commented when her husband and Steven went to get drinks for them. She tilted her head in curiosity. "Hmm, I guess you two were really getting to know each other, huh?"

Wearing a look of innocence, Cherise murmured, "I don't have a clue as to what you mean."

"Uh-huh," Elle responded. "Tell that to someone who will believe you. Just a hint — you might want to put on some more lipstick."

"Okay, he did kiss me," Cherise whispered. She stole a quick look over her shoulder to see if Brennen and Steven were still at the bar.

"I'm not surprised. The man can't seem to keep his eyes off you.

Cherise nodded. "I know one thing. He's a good kisser."

"Okay, that I didn't really need to know," Elle murmured.

"I hope this doesn't sound insane to you, but I'm crazy about him. I'm not thinking of rushing into anything. I'm just taking it one day at a time. I'm going to enjoy being with him on the ship, and when the cruise is over — I guess we'll just have to wait and see what happens."

Steven was bursting with desire. He wanted to take Cherise back to his suite and make love to her, but he knew her well enough to know that she wasn't about casual flings. His body was so on fire for her that he'd had to take a cold shower as soon as he returned to his suite.

While he showered, Steven sorted his feelings for Cherise. She seemed almost perfect in his estimation. She was beautiful, intelligent and honest. If his mother and aunt were here they would agree that Cherise was perfect for him.

No drama and no secrets. Nothing like his last relationship.

CHAPTER 4

The dark and gloomy fortress of Castel Nuovo was their first view of Naples, leaving the port by coach. They continued past Piazza della Borsa. Naples, Italy, was everything Cherise had ever imagined and more.

The coach stopped at Piazza Plebiscito, where she and Steven walked hand in hand, following members of her family and other cruise passengers to view the seventeenth century Royal Palace, the San Carlo Opera House and the Church of St. Francis.

"Have you ever been to Italy before?" she asked Steven.

"No, this is my first time. I'd like to see Rome the next time I come."

"Elle and Brennen visited Rome last year," Cherise said. "She said it was beautiful, and the perfect place for someone who loves shoes."

Steven broke into a grin. "Are you that person?"

"I confess," Cherise said with a smile. "I love shoes."

He turned on his camera. "Go over there. I want to take pictures of you."

She did as he requested. "You're next," Cherise told him.

Steven took several photographs of the Ransom family with the Church of St. Francis serving as the backdrop.

A couple of times, Cherise caught him staring at her. She wondered what he was thinking during those times but couldn't summon the courage to ask him.

They enjoyed refreshments at a local café before getting back on the coach for the return to the ship.

On the way back to the boat, they passed by Mergellina and Castle of the Egg in Santa Lucia.

"Have your family been giving you a hard time about me?" Steven asked her, later that evening. They had decided to have dinner alone at one of the restaurants on the ship.

Cherise smiled. "Not really."

"That's good. I know that we've spent most of this cruise together — I'm not complaining, but this was supposed to be a family trip for you."

"Ivy and I are the only ones not coupled off, so meeting you has been great for me."

Steven eyed her. "You're so incredible."

Cherise grinned. "I'm just me, Steven."

"It's just a relief for me to meet a woman with no drama. I find your honesty so refreshing."

"Sounds like your last relationship was a total trip," Cherise commented. She'd definitely had her share of bad ones too.

"It was," Steven admitted. "I found out that she was married to some man in northern California. We were together for almost a year. I hate secrets."

Cherise chewed on her bottom lip. Steven noticed he had not seen her do that until now.

She had suddenly grown quiet, prompting him to ask her, "You okay?"

She nodded. "I'm just not as hungry as I thought."

Steven studied her. "Are you sure everything is fine?"

Cherise reached over and covered his hand with her own, sending tremors of desire through his body. "I'm fine. I think my body's just winding down from all the walking we did earlier. I hope you don't mind if I renege on our plans to go dancing. I'm just not feeling up to it tonight."

"No, not at all," Steven responded. "I understand completely."

She gave him a small smile. "Thank you."

They left the restaurant a few minutes later, and Steven escorted her to the suite.

"Good night," she said.

Steven pulled her into his arms, kissing her.

She responded hungrily. When they parted, she asked him, "Would you like to have breakfast with me?"

He nodded. "I can't think of anything else I'd rather do. Sleep well."

Steven considered going back to Moonstone's, a club featuring live entertainment, but decided to call it a night. It wouldn't be the same without Cherise.

Cherise paced back and forth in her bedroom.

Spending time with Steven these past few days had been so perfect. She had strong feelings for him, and for a brief moment she'd allowed herself to consider that they might be able to continue seeing each other once they were back in Los Angeles.

That all changed when Steven announced how he hated secrets. What would he think about the one she was carrying around?

She didn't have a husband hidden away, but it was something she never wanted him to find out about her. For years she'd tried to keep it buried deep, but every now and then something would happen to bring it back to the forefront of her mind.

"I've done everything to make up for what happened all those years ago," she whispered. "As much as I care for Steven, this is not something I can ever share with him."

Cherise sat down on the edge of her bed, chewing on her bottom lip. She picked up a pillow, holding it close to her chest.

"I'm falling in love with you, but this is one part of my life that I can't share with you. Not ever."

She pretended to be asleep when Ivy and the girls entered the suite. Cherise just wanted time alone to deal with her troubled thoughts. If given the chance, she would've done things so differently, but there were no do-over's in life.

Steven walked forward, pausing in front of Cherise as they strolled around the ship. "These last few days have flown by. I can't believe this is the last night of our cruise."

Cherise nodded. "Tomorrow we go back to our lives." They stopped at a gift shop's perfume and cosmetics counter. She picked up a sample of Italian cologne, sprayed a little on her left hand and sniffed. "I've had a really good time. It was a great vacation

— partly because I met you." She placed the bottle back on the counter, then picked up another and sprayed cologne on her other hand. "Do you like the way this one smells?"

Steven sniffed her arm. "It smells nice. Reminds me of peaches," he responded.

Cherise turned away from the perfume counter, eying him. "So what happens between you and me when we leave the ship tomorrow?" she asked him.

"We both live in Los Angeles, so I don't see why we can't continue spending time together," Steven responded. "Unless you're not interested in dating me. Are you?"

Her eyebrows rose in amazement. His question had caught her off guard, but she warmed under the look he gave her. "Of course I'd like to keep seeing you."

Steven gave her a smile that sent her pulses racing. "That's exactly what I hoped you'd say," he confessed as he wrapped his arms around her. "I don't want whatever we have to end."

"I don't either," Cherise admitted, giddy with happiness. "I never expected to meet someone like you on the cruise. To be honest, I wasn't even going to come, but Ivy and Elle talked me into it."

"We were supposed to meet," Steven said.

"Do you really believe that?" she questioned.

He nodded. "I'm so glad that I don't have to deal with drama."

"Same here, but Steven," she said with a chuckle, "I'm not perfect. Things are great between us, but I'm sure we're going to have some times when we disagree on whatever."

"As long as we're always honest with each other, we're going to be fine," Steven responded. "My aunt used to always tell me that two people who care about each other should never have secrets."

Cherise kept her expression blank. "You've mentioned your aunt a few times. You must be very close to her."

Steven nodded. "I am. I can't wait for you to meet her. I hope they come home soon."

"You said that they live in Ghana, right?"

"My uncle has a job there. He and Aunt Eula Mae have been in Ghana for ten years now, but he's supposed to be retiring soon. My aunt wants to come home."

Cherise wrapped her arms around him. "Family is everything, isn't it?"

"See, this is why we belong together. You and I have so much in common, including our love for family."

His mouth beckoned her and Cherise was

unable to resist. She pulled his face down to hers, planting a kiss on his lips.

"I want you so much that I can't think right," he whispered hoarsely.

"I want you too," she responded. "But . . ."

Steven nodded. "You're right. I don't want to rush things between us either."

"So what do we do now?" she asked him.

"Join the rest of your family," he suggested. "That should keep us out of trouble. It won't stop me from thinking about making love to you, but I certainly won't act on it."

"What? You're worried about the men in my family?"

"More like the women. Especially Ivy. That woman is no joke."

Cherise laughed. "You got that right."

He kissed her, then said, "C'mon, let's go join the others."

Cherise's body ached for Steven's touch. She stole a peek at the handsome man beside her and smiled.

CHAPTER 5

Two days after the cruise ended, Cherise invited Steven over for dinner. She had been looking forward to seeing him again. Once they returned home and back to work, Steven had to clear his desk to stay on task with his outstanding projects and Cherise had some pressing matters to handle as well.

He arrived promptly at seven.

Cherise threw open the door and stepped back to let Steven enter her house. She'd purchased the home three years ago and was very proud of how much effort she'd put into making it reflect her personality by utilizing warm earth-tone colors.

Leaning into him, Cherise welcomed his warm embrace.

"I'm so glad to see you, sweetheart," he murmured in her hair. "I want you to know that it was hard to get my work done, because you were on my mind all day long."

Cherise wrapped her arms around him,

and replied, "It was the same for me. At one point I thought this day would never end."

Steven laughed. "I know what you mean. I kept thinking that there had to be something wrong with my watch."

Cherise gestured toward the love seat and said, "Give me a few minutes to set everything up and then we can eat. I was late leaving the office."

"Take your time, sweetheart. We have all evening."

Ten minutes later, Cherise led Steven into the dining room.

He eyed the beautifully decorated table. Vibrant flames flickered from the gold-colored candles, casting a soft glow on the succulent display of chicken, scalloped potatoes, homemade muffins and steaming asparagus. "Everything looks delicious."

"Thank you." Cherise sat down in the chair Steven pulled out for her. He eased into a chair facing her.

After giving thanks, they dug into their food. Cherise smiled when Steven closed his eyes as he chewed. She was pleased to see that he enjoyed the meal. Conversation was kept to a minimum while they ate.

After dinner, Steven helped her with the cleanup, which was definitely a first for her.

None of the men she'd dated in the past ever came into the kitchen unless it was to get something to eat or drink.

Later, curled up on the sofa together, Steven acknowledged, "The roast chicken was good. You are a wonderful cook, Cherise."

She couldn't get enough of looking at him. His brown eyes were lit from within with a golden glow. Cherise found her voice. "I'm glad you enjoyed dinner. The truth is, I was hoping to impress you with my culinary skills."

His eyes clung to hers. "Well, you did. I'm definitely impressed."

"Okay. I need to know if you are for real."

Steven threw back his head and laughed.

"I'm serious, Steven," Cherise said. "I have to be honest with you. You seem almost too good to be true. I guess it didn't matter much when we were on the cruise ship. I thought you'd somehow be different now that we're back home."

"Sweetheart, I'm for real," he responded. "To tell the truth, I was feeling the same way about you, Cherise. I mean, I've never met a woman that I considered perfect for me — not like you are."

"No one has ever treated me the way you do. It's kind of foreign. Do you know what

I mean?"

"I do," he responded. "Cherise, I'm not going to change, if that's what you're worried about."

Moving closer, she laid her head on his chest.

Together, they watched television.

Three hours later, Steven gently sat Cherise up and rose to his feet. "I guess I'd better get going. We both have to work tomorrow."

Cherise stood up too. She still ached for his touch so much, and her feelings for him were intensifying, wrapping around her like a warm blanket. Her emotions melted her resolve. "I don't want you to leave, Steven. I want you to spend the night with me."

"Are you sure about this?" he wanted to know. His steady gaze bored into her in silent expectation.

In response, she led him by the hand to her bedroom. Standing in the middle of the floor, they undressed each other in silence.

Steven held her in his arms, his gaze making passionate love to her. Taking in his powerful presence, she asked, "What is it?"

"I've grown to care deeply for you." Pausing, he gazed at her. "I knew you were special from the first time I ever saw you."

Cherise was moved by his words. "I feel

the same way about you."

"I'm not running games, sweetheart," Steven stated. "I know it sounds like I'm moving fast, but you are everything I ever wanted in a woman. The reason I'm telling you this is because I want you to know where you stand with me before we fall into bed. I'm not looking for casual sex."

Cherise didn't really know how to respond. "I-I really don't know what to say. I never expected this."

"I have to ask. How do you feel about me, Cherise?" He regarded her with a speculative gaze. "Are you looking for something more?"

He looked almost afraid of her response.

Stroking his cheek, she murmured, "I want a real relationship, Steven."

Cherise watched the play of emotions on his face.

Steven swept her, weightless, into his arms and carried her to the bed. After placing her in the middle of the bed, he crawled in behind her.

Cherise could feel his uneven breathing on her cheek as he held her close. The touch of his hand was almost unbearable in its tenderness. His mouth covered hers hungrily, leaving her mouth burning with fire.

The touch of her lips on his sent a shock

70

wave through his entire body with a savage intensity. Steven planted kisses on her shoulders, neck and face. As he roused her passion, his own need grew stronger.

Passion pounded the blood through her heart, chest and head, causing Cherise to breathe in deep, soul-drenching drafts. She had never been as happy as she was in this moment in time, and she didn't want it to end.

Cherise watched the rise and fall of Steven's chest as he slept, thinking about what had transpired earlier. He made her feel loved in the way that he touched her, kissed her and held her in his arms.

She closed her eyes, seeking sleep, but images from her past resurfaced, forcing her to stay wide awake. Cherise shook her head, trying to shake the turbulent thoughts away.

Steven placed a protective arm around her, pulling her closer to him. He never opened his eyes.

She felt a thread of guilt at the thought of keeping secrets from the man she was falling in love with. Steven was right — there shouldn't be any secrets between you and that special someone. However, she didn't believe she needed to tell him about every aspect of her life.

What happened in the past stays in the past, Cherise decided. She was a different person now, more mature and self-assured. Life was good. She had a wonderful family and a good man.

It was time to bury the past once and for all.

She stretched and yawned, waking Steven.

"Hey, baby," he mumbled.

"Go back to sleep," Cherise whispered. She snuggled up against him.

Steven planted kisses on her forehead, her cheeks and neck, sending delicious spirals down her body.

They made love a second time.

Cherise fell asleep, but was awakened an hour later by thoughts of her secret one night ten years ago. The night she and some friends decided to break into what they thought was an empty house. She was fifteen at the time, overweight and willing to do just about anything to be accepted by her friends. None of them expected someone to be inside the house.

A woman came toward them swinging a bat. Everything happened so fast that night. One of the boys she was with hit the woman, knocking her unconscious.

Cherise winced at the memory.

The others ran away, but she stayed

behind. Scared that the woman was seriously hurt, Cherise called 9-1-1 before rushing from the house, wanting to forget that night forever.

Steven and his parents were having dinner the next day, and he invited Cherise to join them. He wanted her to meet his mother in particular, because she was able to read people like books. She had a wonderful gift of discernment.

"I don't know if I'm ready to meet your parents," Cherise told him.

He studied her for a moment. "Okay, I thought we were on the same page. Was I wrong?"

She shook her head. "I was under the impression that we'd be taking things slow."

"It's just dinner with me and my parents, Cherise. I wanted them to meet you."

She folded her arms across her chest. "Why?"

He met her gaze. "Cherise, I have feelings for you. I can't really put a name to them yet, but I know that I like being with you. We have a lot in common. I like that you are straightforward, you don't play games — at least not that I can tell. You're ambitious, intelligent, beautiful . . . what more can I say?"

"Sometimes I feel like you have me on this pedestal, Steven. I'm not perfect. I do mess up from time to time."

"We all do," he said. "But that doesn't change the fact that you take my breath away every time I see you. When you smile, my heart does this little flip."

Cherise broke into a grin. "Steven, you are such a romantic."

He pulled her to him. "I don't want to rush you into anything, sweetheart. Let me know if I'm being too pushy."

She kissed him. "I will."

"So what about dinner with my parents?"

"I would love to meet them," Cherise responded. "Now I need to get to work and so do you."

He followed her outside.

"I'll pick you up at six-thirty," he told Cherise.

She climbed into her SUV and followed Steven to the freeway.

Cherise hummed softly to the music playing on the radio. The song ended, and a news report about a recent break-in put a damper on her mood. She wondered what Steven would say if she told him that she and her friends had attacked some poor woman in her home when she was fifteen? Although she never struck the woman, she still felt just as responsible. She was pretty sure that Steven wouldn't think she was so perfect if he knew her secret shame.

CHAPTER 6

Cherise hadn't been in her office ten minutes when the secretary buzzed her to say, "Maxie would like to see you. Can you come to her office now?"

"Sure."

She pushed away from her desk, got up and left her office.

Cherise stopped outside of her supervisor's door to straighten her clothing. Dark brown eyes closed, she whispered a quick prayer before entering the huge office, saying, "Maxie, you wanted to see me?"

An older woman with salt-and-pepper hair peered over her bifocals and nodded. "Come on in, Cherise."

Easing into one of the visitor's chairs, she sat down, looking across the huge oak desk at the reed-thin woman sitting there.

Tapping her foot impatiently, Cherise waited for Maxie to complete her notes.

Finally laying the pen aside, Maxie Sheppard settled back into the high-backed chair that seemed to swallow her. Smiling warmly, she asked, "I've been in and out of the office so much, you never did tell me how you enjoyed your cruise."

"It was wonderful," Cherise said. "In fact, I met someone on the ship. He lives here in Los Angeles."

"Really? Have you two kept in touch?"

She nodded. "We've been seeing each other since the cruise ended. He's an architect with Lawson, Hendricks and Sampson."

"I'm happy for you," Maxie said with a sincere smile. "Well, the reason I wanted to see you is because I know how much you wanted the senior counselor position. Are you still interested?"

Sitting up straight, Cherise almost shouted her answer. "Yes."

Maxie smiled. "I'm happy to inform you that it's yours, then. You've got the position."

Cherise could barely contain her excitement. All her dreams were coming true. "Thank you so much, Maxie. You have no idea how much I wanted this promotion. Thank you."

"You can move into your new office today, if you'd like."

"I think I'll do just that. Thank you so much, Maxie. I really appreciate it." Cherise was almost giddy with happiness.

"Let's get something clear. I didn't *give* it to you," Maxie stated. "Cherise, you've earned it. You've been here at the Darlene Sheppard Center for a few years now. All the kids here love you, and so does the rest of the staff. You're good at your job and with the girls."

"It's because I understand how those kids feel, Maxie. I've been there." Cherise paused a moment before continuing. "I wish there had been a center like this when I was growing up — a place where overweight kids can wear swimsuits with pride, or just have fun without others picking on them. I remember when I used to go swimming how some of the children used to follow me, yelling, 'Fat! You're so fat, it looks like you're wearing a slingshot.' "

"After my daughter committed suicide . . ." Maxie shook her head sadly. "I knew I had to do something. The thing is, Darlene was a normal twelve-year-old. Not skinny like me, but certainly not what I'd call obese either — Darlene just thought she was fat, and the other kids wouldn't stop teasing her . . . She tried so hard to lose the weight over the summer and she did lose thirty pounds, but when she went back that fall they still made jokes. She hanged herself in the closet."

Maxie swiped at her wet eyes. "I don't want another mother or another child to suffer the way my daughter and I did."

"Children can be so cruel, and unfortunately we tend to believe what others say about us. Good or bad."

Maxie nodded her head emphatically. "Yes, they can. But at least we're doing something to help. My daughter will not have died for nothing."

Feeling her supervisor's heartache, Cherise sought to comfort her. "You're a very special woman, Maxie. It takes courage to do what you did in Darlene's memory."

"I wish you could've met my daughter and talked to her. Maybe . . ." Maxie fell back against her chair, sighing. "I guess it's no use thinking like that. I'll meet with you in the morning, and we'll go over your new duties in detail."

"If it hadn't been for you, the kids wouldn't have a place like this. Darlene would be so proud of you." Cherise stood up and strolled over to the door. She was about to leave when she heard Maxie call her name.

"Congratulations on your promotion."

Smiling, Cherise replied, "Thank you."

Leaving Maxie's office, she practically skipped down the hall.

When Cherise got to her office, she found a young girl of sixteen waiting outside her door. "Hi, Bridgett."

Following her into the office, Bridgett murmured a soft hello.

Puzzled, Cherise glanced down at her appointment book. "Did we have an appointment this afternoon?"

Her voice barely above a whisper, Bridgett replied, "Naw, I just came by to talk. Are you real busy right now?" She stood near the door as if ready to bolt at any given moment.

Seating herself behind the desk, Cherise motioned to a nearby chair. "Have a seat. I have a few minutes to talk." She leaned back and asked, "What's going on?"

With her head bowed, Bridgett mumbled, "Nothing much going on. I just . . . felt like talkin' to you." A half smile crossed her face. "You said I could come to you whenever I needed to talk. So I came."

"I'm glad." Cherise could see pain etched on the young girl's chubby face. "Are those girls still teasing you?"

Looking down at her hands, Bridgett responded, "Yeah, but that's never gonna end. They don't like me 'cause I'm fat."

"Bridgett, sweetheart, don't let those girls get to you. If you ignore them, they'll soon find someone else to bother."

"It's just that . . . they're right, Miss Ransom. I am fat and I'm ugly!" A solitary tear slid down her ginger-brown cheek. Bridgett hastily wiped it away with the back of her hand.

Cherise's heart went out to the teenager. She remembered what it was like to be the butt of jokes, to be overweight and wanting so much to be liked by her peers. She leaned forward. "Let's get something clear, Bridgett. *You are not ugly.* I think you are one of the most beautiful young women I've ever met. But my telling you this won't make the hurt go away. *You have to believe it.*"

Bridgett weighed Cherise with a critical squint. "Th-That's e-easy for you to say. Look at you. You're not fat."

"I'm not thin either. I'm a size fourteen and proud of it. I used to weigh two-hundred fifty pounds when I was your age," she announced.

Bridgett's round eyes opened wider. "*You* were fat?" She shook her head in disbelief. "Naw!"

Cherise nodded. "Yes, I was fat. My

classmates used to laugh at me all the time. They used to make crude jokes about me. They would shout for everybody to hide their lunches when I walked into the room." Hot tears burned her eyes from the memory.

"So, what did you do?"

Cherise was quiet for a minute determined to void the pain and heartache of the past. "I wanted so badly to be popular, I did whatever my so-called friends wanted me to. One night I got into some serious trouble. It was then that I decided I didn't want those kinds of friends." She paused for a minute. "I moved away, started exercising and watching what I ate. I lost some of the weight."

"That must have made you really happy."

"Not really," Cherise admitted. "Instead of being thrilled at having lost weight, I found myself becoming angry. The underlying message was that I was making my body conform more to society's idea of how I should look. As if it were one of the best things I could do as a woman. It was as if losing the weight made me part of the real world. Like being a big girl made me a freak."

Nodding, Bridgett agreed. "That's the way I feel now. Especially when people laugh at me, and I see those commercials where women brag about how much weight they've lost — they act like their new bodies are brand-new cars." She sucked her teeth. "They make me sick."

Cherise's mouth quirked with amusement. "What I've learned over the years is that being a full-figured woman doesn't make me a bad person. Being dark-skinned doesn't make me bad either. It only makes me an individual. So I'm not one of those skinny women all over TV and magazines. I may never have men drool over my body, but that's okay, too. These are things I have no control over. Once I realized that particular truth, I became my own cheerleader."

"Huh?"

"I learned to love me, Bridgett," Cherise explained. "Once I did that, I learned to pick my friends, not the other way around. So what if I'm not popular? Or have light skin or the body of a model? I'm still a nice person." Grinning, she stated, "The way I see it, there's just a lot more of me to love."

Hope sprang into Bridgett's eyes. "Do you think I can lose some of this weight? Like you did? I know I won't ever be thin, but I do want to lose some of this fat."

"I believe you can do anything you want. You just have to want it bad enough,

Bridgett. You've only got to believe in yourself."

Cherise smiled and handed the young girl a tissue. "But understand that you don't have to change yourself to please your friends. If they can't accept you for who you are, then change your friends. Don't let those other kids get to you."

"I won't. Thank you, Miss Ransom." Bridgett beamed happily as she stood up to leave. "I guess I'll let you get back to work."

"Come talk to me anytime."

"I will." Bridgett smiled and closed the door.

Cherise leaned back into her chair feeling whole and complete. She hoped and prayed that Bridgett's low self-esteem would not lead her down the same road hers had led her. The loud ringing of her telephone interrupted her reverie. Picking up the phone, she announced, "Cherise speaking."

"Hello, honey. How's your day going?" Steven's voice held a rasp of excitement.

She felt her heart race with anticipation over hearing Steven's low, baritone voice. "It's so good to hear from you," Cherise said. "My day is going great. What about yours?"

"It would be better if I were spending my time with you," he said huskily. "I can't wait to see you."

Her heart skipped a beat. Lowering her voice, Cherise whispered into the phone saying, "I'm looking forward to seeing you, too. We've got a lot of celebrating to do tonight."

"Oh, yeah? So what are we celebrating?"

Cherise could no longer keep her news to herself. "I got a promotion at work. I'm the new senior counselor."

"Honey, that's great. Congratulations."

"This is my year, baby. I can feel it." Cherise talked with Steven a few minutes more before hanging up.

She strolled gaily down the hall toward her new corner office.

Cherise stood in the room visualizing her artwork and desk accessories in there. She rubbed her fingers across the red-brown-stained desk as she sank down into the swivel chair. "I'm going to have to adjust the height on this," she murmured to herself.

She glanced up at the wall clock and decided to postpone her move into her new office until tomorrow. Today she needed to leave the office right at five in order to be ready by the time Steven picked her up.

Cherise silently counted her blessings. She was dating a wonderful man and had just gotten a promotion she desperately wanted. The way things were going for her, Cherise was positive that nothing could destroy her happiness.

"Aunt Eula Mae, I can't wait for you to meet Cherise. She's a really nice girl." Steven shifted the phone from one side to the other. "Mom's meeting her tonight. We're having dinner with her and Dad."

"Isn't this a little soon?"

Steven frowned. "I don't think so."

"Hon, you just met the girl a few weeks ago. What do you really know about her?" Eula Mae asked.

"I know that Cherise comes from a very large family, and that she loves working with teens. She's beautiful and intelligent, and there's no drama. We don't have any secrets between us. She understands family loyalty."

"She does sound perfect, I guess."

"When you meet her, you'll see what I mean, Aunt Eula Mae. Cherise and I are not rushing into anything, but we are trying to build something here. I'm ready to settle down and so is she."

"Well, I look forward to meeting her."

They talked a few minutes more before ending the call. The opinions of his mother and his aunt carried a lot of weight with

Steven. They both possessed strong discerning spirits which had kept him out of harm's way throughout his life.

Steven was sure they would both see Cherise through his eyes.

Steven arrived promptly at six.

As they headed to the car, she mumbled, "I hope your parents will like me."

"They will." He reached for her hand. "Honey, you have nothing to worry about. They're going to love you."

Cherise laughed. "I'll settle for them just liking me." She still couldn't believe that she was already meeting his parents. Usually she was in a relationship for months before the man ever took her to meet his mother and father.

She climbed into the car.

Steven shut her door and strolled around the car to the driver's side. Soon they were on their way.

His parents were already at the restaurant when they arrived thirty minutes later. Steven made the introductions.

Rebecca Chambers embraced her as if she was a member of the family. "Cherise, it's so nice to meet you. We've heard all about you."

She glanced over at Steven then back to

his mother. "Really?"

Rebecca nodded. "He's talked nonstop about you since he's been back. I'm glad you were able to join us tonight so that we could get to know you." Her smile was genuine.

They were seated a few minutes later.

After the waiter brought their drinks, he took their orders.

Cherise was amazed at how quickly he returned with their appetizers.

They bowed their heads as Steven's father said the blessing.

Munching on a mini crab cake, Cherise listened to Steven discuss his plans for the new church building.

"It never fails. Men talk about sports, women and their jobs," Rebecca teased.

Cherise burst into laughter along with Steven and his father. She liked these people a lot and enjoyed their good-natured bantering.

The waiter arrived to refill their drinks.

"Cherise, you have to join us for dinner one Sunday after church," Steven Sr. said. "My wife makes a killer roast. That's how she got me, you know?"

Rebecca shot him a look. "I heard that, old man."

Steven Sr. awarded his wife with a large

grin. "Woman, you know it's true. Your mama told you that the way to a man's heart was through his stomach. That's why you tried to feed me every time I came around."

Cherise bit back her laughter when Rebecca playfully pinched her husband's arm.

Steven leaned over, whispering, "They're always talking like that to each other."

"They are so funny," she whispered back. "It's clear they adore each other, though."

Their entrées arrived.

"I spoke to Aunt Eula Mae earlier today," Steven announced. "She really wants to come home. Uncle Jerome's retirement party is in a couple of months, but she's ready to come home now."

"My poor sister's tired of Ghana," Rebecca said.

"I'll be glad when she comes home." Steven took a sip of water and swallowed. "I really miss her."

Rebecca laughed. "I'm sure you do." She explained to Cherise, "My sister is Steven's other mother. Those two are close as peas in a pod."

Wiping her mouth on the corner of a napkin, Cherise eyed Steven and smiled. "I think that's really sweet."

"Are you close to your family, Cherise?"

Rebecca asked.

Before she could respond, Steven said, "You should have seen them on the ship — there were over fifty cruising with us. They're all very close."

Rebecca smiled. "I think that's wonderful. Eula Mae and I have always been close. I guess it's because we were the only girls out of seven children."

"My family and I enjoy being together, but we enjoy being away from each other, too," Cherise confessed. "The clan can be overwhelming at times, but when one is in trouble, we're all there for each other."

"That's how family should be," Rebecca said.

After dinner, Steven and Cherise went back to his place.

"Your parents are wonderful," she told him as they walked into the living room. "I had a nice time."

"They enjoyed meeting you, Cherise. Now I can't wait for you to meet my aunt. She's my heart. If anybody messes with her, they have to deal with me."

Steven slipped an arm around her as they settled back to watch a movie. Throughout the movie, she and Steven shot furtive glances at each other.

Cherise knew what he was thinking because it echoed her own thoughts.

When the movie ended, Steven and Cherise rose to their feet. He lifted her face up to him. "Come here and kiss me."

Cherise met his lips with her own. Her heart fluttered at his touch.

"Why don't we take this upstairs?"

In response, Steven led the way to his bedroom.

Cherise released a soft gasp upon seeing the huge bouquet of roses lying on a small table beside an ice bucket with a chilled bottle of champagne.

"I wanted to celebrate your promotion," Steven whispered in her ear. "I also have strawberries and cheese and crackers prepared. You stay here and make yourself comfortable while I go get them."

Cherise turned in his arms. "You are so good to me, Steven."

He planted a kiss on her forehead. "I'll be right back. Oh, there's a gift on the bed for you. I hope you like it."

Steven left the room, while Cherise rushed to find out what was in the beautifully wrapped package.

Cherise was standing in the center of the bedroom wearing the sexy black lingerie Steven had purchased for her when he returned.

He looked awestruck for a moment.

"Are you going to say something?"

Steven placed the platter of food on the table, picked up his pad and began drawing. "I want to capture this look, sweetheart. You are the most beautiful woman I've ever met."

He dropped down into a nearby chair.

Cherise opened her mouth to speak, but he stopped her by saying, "Just stand there . . . like that. I'm almost done with your face. We can do the rest later."

Steven sketched furiously, his brow furrowed as he worked.

He stood up and showed her the drawing.

"It's beautiful," Cherise said with a smile. "I can't wait to see it when it's finished. I'm amazed at your talent. You could've been an artist painting some of the architectural masterpieces all over the world."

"I could never settle for just painting them," Steven confessed. "They inspire me to create my own designs. They inspire me." His gaze met hers. "*You* inspire me."

Steven poured champagne into two flutes and handed one to Cherise. She picked up a strawberry and dropped it into hers before sipping from it. He did the same.

"The perfect way to end a perfect day," Cherise murmured.

They finished off their champagne.

Steven kissed Cherise, holding her close to him.

They parted long enough to undress.

"This will be the perfect ending for a perfect day," he told her as he picked her up and carried her over to the bed.

CHAPTER 7

"Since I've met your parents, I guess it's time for you to come to one of the Ransom family dinners," Cherise told Steven over breakfast the next day.

"Ransom family dinner? Is this something huge?"

"It's a clan tradition." Cherise retrieved a bowl of grapes from the refrigerator. "We get together every month at my aunt Amanda's house. You know, she and I have a relationship that's very similar to the one you share with your aunt."

Steven stuck a forkful of scrambled eggs into his mouth. After swallowing, he said, "I'd love to go with you. It sounds like fun."

"Bring some clothes with you to play ball in. We'll go out there this Sunday, if you don't already have plans." Cherise bit into a grape.

"My plans are to spend my day with you." Steven wiped his mouth on a napkin and then took a long sip of his coffee.

They cleaned up the kitchen area before leaving the house. Steven dropped Cherise off at her house before heading downtown to his office.

Humming to herself, Cherise changed into a pair of black pants and a pink silk shirt. She pulled her hair back into a ponytail, grabbed her purse and headed back out.

She pulled into the parking lot beside the center almost twenty minutes before her scheduled start time. Cherise strolled into the center, grinning from ear to ear.

She walked into her new office and sat down at the desk. Cherise couldn't be happier with the way her life was going at the moment.

Her telephone rang, cutting into her thoughts.

"Hey, where have you been?" Elle asked when she answered. "I called you a couple of times at home last night, and I tried your cell. You had me worried."

"I'm sorry. I spent the night with Steven," Cherise announced. "We were celebrating and didn't want to be disturbed, so I turned off my phone."

"Celebrating?" Elle repeated. "Celebrating what?"

"I got a promotion here at work. I'm the

95

new senior counselor."

"That's wonderful, Cherise. I knew you would get it."

Cherise smiled. "You kept telling me that, but I didn't want to get my hopes up."

"Congratulations, cousin." Elle paused for a heartbeat before commenting, "So you and Steven have taken your relationship to another level, I see."

"Things are going so well with us," Cherise said. "At times, it almost seems too good to be true, but I've decided to just enjoy the time we have together."

"You love him, don't you?"

"I do," Cherise admitted.

"Do you think he feels the same way?"

"I hope so, Elle, but Steven and I haven't mentioned the L-word yet. I think we're both determined not to make any mistakes." Cherise chuckled. "Either that or he's waiting for his parents and this aunt he talks about all the time to give their approval."

"Sounds like a close family too."

"Just like us."

Cherise and Elle made plans to have lunch one day next week before ending their conversation.

She spent most of her day moving files from one office to the other.

Steven surprised Cherise when he showed

up in her doorway at noon.

"What are you doing here?"

"I knew that you would be busy moving into your new office, and since I have a meeting later this afternoon right down the street from here, I figured I'd take you out to lunch."

Cherise smiled. "I was thinking about ordering a sandwich, but now that you're here, I'm not going to miss an opportunity to spend time with you."

"Speaking of time," Steven said as he sat down in one of the visitor chairs. "I have to go on a business trip next week. I'll be gone for five days."

"Wow, I'm going to really miss you," Cherise said. "Where are you going?"

"I have to go to Chicago for a conference."

"When do you leave?"

"Monday morning," Steven answered. "I'll be back Saturday afternoon."

They left the center and drove to a nearby restaurant for lunch.

"Are you all packed up?" Steven inquired as they waited for their entrées to arrive.

Cherise nodded. "I actually got a lot done. I hope to be settled in before I leave this evening."

Steven was staring at her.

"Why do you do that?" she asked.

"What am I doing?"

"Sometimes you just stare at me."

Steven chuckled. "I never tire of looking at you."

"Why are you still single?" Cherise wanted to know. "I can't imagine any woman letting someone like you just walk out of her life."

"My last girlfriend was married. I didn't know it at the time. He worked in Sacramento, so I guess that's why it never dawned on me. My mother didn't care for her — she kept telling me that something didn't seem right with this woman. My aunt said the same thing. Aunt Eula never met her, but they did talk on the phone and e-mail. Well, they were right."

"I assure you that I don't have a husband hidden away anywhere."

He smiled. "I'm so glad to hear that."

Their food arrived.

"What was your last relationship like?" Steven asked.

"He was a major jerk," Cherise said. She wiped her mouth on the edge of her napkin. "He was very critical of my weight and just about everything I did, so I told him to find someone who actually made him happy. I also told him that it was going to be hard dating himself."

Steven laughed.

Cherise sampled her pecan-crusted salmon. "This is delicious."

He agreed. "I love the food here. Everything I've tried has been good."

When they finished eating, Steven paid the check and then drove her back to the center.

"Thanks for lunch," Cherise said, then planted a quick kiss on his lips. "Good luck with your meeting."

"I'll call you later on tonight," Steven promised.

Cherise was on cloud nine. She practically floated through the double doors of the center and down the hallway to her office.

That Sunday was dinner with Cherise's family. "This is the house," Cherise said, gesturing for Steven to find an empty space to park.

He pulled in beside a gleaming, black BMW 650i and parked his Chrysler 300, then got out and walked around to the passenger side to open the door for Cherise.

The two-story French-style home was well-kept and striking. He liked the huge Palladian window. Two huge, healthy-looking ferns sat on either side of the front door, welcoming them.

"I lived in this house from the time I was fifteen until I went to college," Cherise said.

"Really? Did your parents live here as well?"

She shook her head. "No. I . . . I needed to get away, so my mom let me come here to stay." Cherise hoped that Steven wouldn't press her for more answers. She couldn't tell him why she'd really left home. That it was because she feared the police would be looking for her after what happened that night.

"Did you and your mother have a fight or something?"

Cherise didn't look him in the eye when she responded, "Something like that."

She released a soft sigh of relief when Kaitlin opened the front door. Steven was left with the men while she joined her aunt and female cousins in the kitchen. Her sister arrived a few minutes later.

"I guess I should've gone on that cruise," she teased. "Then I'd be walking around with a new boo. I wouldn't have time for my sister or anyone else . . ."

Cherise embraced Jazz. "I'm sorry. Why don't we do something together next week?"

"Is Boo going out of town?"

When Cherise didn't respond, everyone

in the kitchen burst into laughter.

"See," Jazz said. "I can't get time with my own sister until Boo goes out of town. That's so wrong."

"I promise I'll do better by you," Cherise told her sister.

Jazz chuckled. "It's okay. I'm just messing with you. You look really happy."

"She does, doesn't she?" her aunt interjected. "I guess this Steven is good for you."

"He's great to me, Aunt Amanda. He treats me like a woman should be treated." Cherise reached for the pitcher to make lemonade. "I really appreciate him because I've had so many jerks in my life."

"I can tell that he really cares about you," Elle said. "I see the way he looks at you."

Cherise grinned. "As far as I'm concerned, he is a keeper."

They had dinner ready twenty minutes later. Kaitlin and Jillian made sure that the tables were set before calling in the children, who were served first. After everyone had plates laden with fried chicken, macaroni and cheese, turnips and corn bread, Laine said the blessing.

Steven had gotten to know everyone on the cruise, so he felt immediately at home. Cherise was pleased that her aunt seemed to like him as well.

After dessert, the men announced they would be cleaning up, which thrilled Cherise and the other women. Steven was given a reprieve, since this was his first visit, but he insisted on helping out.

The men played a round of basketball when they were done.

Cherise sat outside with Kaitlin, Elle and Jazz, cheering them on. She loved seeing Steven in action.

"Boo has some skills," Jazz said. "Cherise, you did good."

"I think so," she responded.

Cherise and Steven stayed another hour before driving back to Los Angeles.

When they entered her house and settled down in the family room, Steven said, "So tell me about your childhood. I want to know what you were like back then."

"Why?" Cherise asked. She didn't like talking about her past. There were things her own family didn't know.

"I just want to know."

Cherise met his gaze. "I don't like talking about the past — there's no point."

A look of confusion passed over his features. "What's so terrible that you can't talk about, Cherise?"

She rose to her feet. "I didn't say there was something that happened. I just don't

102

discuss my past with anyone. I don't see the point. I had a childhood just like everyone else. There were ups and downs."

"Why are you so upset, then?"

"Because you keep pressing the issue," she snapped. "I'm not the same person that I was back then, so let's just drop it."

Steven rose to his feet and walked over to her. "I'm sorry if I upset you."

Cherise took a deep breath. "I shouldn't have snapped at you. I'm sorry."

"I need to get home and finish packing for my trip."

Cherise was disappointed. "I thought you were staying here tonight."

Steven shook his head. "I need to get going."

He was upset with her. Cherise realized that she'd overreacted, but didn't know how to fix it without risking more questions.

She walked him to the door. "Have a safe trip."

He kissed her. "I'll call you after I get there."

Cherise watched him until he got into the car and drove away. "I'm going to miss you so much," she whispered. She hoped that by the time Steven returned he would have forgotten what had happened.

■ ■ ■ ■

Cherise was hiding something, but what? Steven wondered. Why was she so close-mouthed about her youth?

He told himself that it was probably something too tragic for her to talk about, which only made him even more curious. He knew that she had a seemingly good relationship with her parents, although she'd spent much of her teenage years with her aunt.

Steven thought they had grown pretty close over the course of the past couple of months. It bothered him that Cherise was not willing to share her past with him. It wasn't as if he was entitled, but . . . he shook his head. Steven didn't understand it at all.

A thread of apprehension snaked down his spine. Steven tried to shake the feeling. Cherise had every right to her privacy. But he couldn't dismiss the feeling that she was keeping something from him.

Steven took his mind off Cherise for the moment. He needed to finish packing and mentally prepare for the upcoming conference. Maybe they needed this time apart to really sort out their feelings for one another.

Chapter 8

Cherise threw her damp towel on the edge of the huge Jacuzzi tub. She had just enjoyed a nice, hot bubbly bath after coming home from a Pilates class. Being off her feet and soaking in the warmth soothed her aching body and left her feeling clean and totally relaxed.

Steven was scheduled to arrive within the hour, and she was looking forward to seeing him. She had missed him terribly while he was away.

She had just gotten dressed when the doorbell rang.

Why is he here so early? Cherise wondered as she rushed to answer the front door.

"Jazz, what are you doing here?" She stepped aside to let her sister enter the house.

"I came here to see you," she responded. "I was thinking that we could grab something to eat and maybe catch a movie or something."

"Jazz, I'm so sorry. I already have plans. Steven's coming home today," Cherise told her. "Can we do it to tomorrow night?"

"That's fine," Jazz responded with a shrug. "I'll give Ivy a call and see if she wants to hang."

"How do I look?" Cherise asked, twirling around slowly. She had chosen a slinky maxi dress in a turquoise color to wear with black accessories and turquoise-and-black shoes.

Jazz smiled at her and said, "Beautiful as always. You'd better be glad that I can't wear your clothes."

Cherise chuckled. Jazz was a skinny little thing and always complained about her weight. She wanted to be a couple of dress sizes bigger because she thought it wouldn't make her look so anorexic, the way she looked now.

Steven arrived just as Jazz was leaving. "You two have fun," she told them.

"Why are you looking at me like that?" Cherise asked when she caught him staring at her.

Steven covered her hand with his own. "Because I can't believe how lucky I am. There aren't many women like you. You're as rare as each new day. No two are alike."

Her lips turned upward. Steven always

had a way of saying just the right thing to her. This is why she loved this man.

"I missed you, Cherise. I'd gotten so used to seeing you every day. It was hard."

"I really missed you, too."

They sat down in the family room.

"So how did your conference go?" Cherise asked.

"Fine," he responded. "I ran into a couple of friends from college. I hadn't seen them since we graduated. We had a great time catching up."

"That's wonderful," she said. She couldn't help but wonder if any of them were female. She didn't ask, because she didn't want to come off like a jealous lover.

Steven wrapped an arm around her. "Most of the time, I kept thinking about how much I wanted to see you."

She gave him a sidelong glance. "Is that why you only called me twice?"

He laughed. "I was in workshops most of the day and then in the evenings, I —"

"You don't have to explain anything to me, Steven," she quickly interjected. "I'm just messing with you."

"While I was away from you, I realized something."

"What's that?" Cherise asked.

"I know that something must have happened in your past that you can't talk about and initially it bothered me . . ."

"Steven," she began.

He held up his hand to quiet her. "Let me finish, please."

"Okay."

"I want you to know that when you're ready, you can tell me anything. I won't judge you." Steven took her hand in his and said, "Cherise, I'm in love with you."

She looked into his beautiful brown eyes. "I love you, too. Honey, I need you to understand something. I spent too many years looking back, and I just don't want to do that anymore."

Cherise leaned over and kissed him, wanting to put an end to any more conversation. Her mother had always told her that actions speak much louder than words.

Since the night they'd declared their love for one another a month ago, Steven felt as if he and Cherise had grown much closer. In the past couple of days, he had been thinking more and more about marriage.

He wanted to marry Cherise.

Steven checked his watch. It was almost lunchtime. He pushed away from his desk and rose to his feet. He needed to make one stop before grabbing a bite to eat.

He placed a call to Cherise while still in the parking garage.

"Hey, baby."

"Steven, hello."

"I know you're busy, so I won't keep you. I'd like to take you to dinner tonight."

"How about I cook instead?" Cherise suggested.

"Sure, if you don't mind."

"Of course I don't mind," she said. "I'll make it very romantic."

"Perfect," he murmured. "I'll see you tonight, sweetheart."

Steven ended the call and put away his cell phone.

He stopped at the jewelry store four blocks away. Steven was inside for only fifteen minutes. From there, he picked up a sandwich and drove back to his office.

Steven decided to make it a short lunch so that he could leave work a half hour early.

Time seemed to move at a snail's pace.

He kept watching the clock, silently urging it to speed up. He was ready to get off work. Tonight was going to be a big night for him and Cherise. He had a very important question for her, and for the first time in a very long time, he was scared.

Steven left the building promptly at five-thirty, singing softly.

He rushed home, showered and changed. Said a quick prayer and left for Cherise's house.

She greeted him at the door with a huge smile when he arrived.

Her smile was the only encouragement Steven needed. "You look beautiful," he complimented. The black strappy dress Cherise was wearing really flattered her figure.

They sat down at the dining room table.

Steven hoped Cherise couldn't tell just how nervous he was all through dinner. He hardly touched his meal because he was too excited to eat.

He had never been this nervous in his life.

Cherise was watching him, studying his expression. "Steven? Is something wrong? Did I cook the steak too long?" Pointing to his plate, she added, "I notice you haven't really eaten much."

He glanced up at her, one hand fingering the small velvet box in his pocket. "Nothing's wrong, sweetheart. The food is fine. I'm just not real hungry. We'll put it away and I'll eat it later."

Her eyes never left his face. "Are you sure?"

Clasping his hands together, he said, "Cherise, I have something I want to talk to you about. Something I want to ask you."

She leaned closer. "What is it?"

This was it. Steven took a deep breath. He had considered waiting until Christmas, which was two months away, or Valentine's Day, but decided not to wait.

Steven swallowed hard, and then said, "Cherise, we've been together three months, but it feels like we're known each other for much longer. I think that I've loved you from the first moment I laid eyes on you. It just took some time for me to realize it."

He suddenly felt unsure of himself. Cherise must have sensed this because she reached out and covered his hand with her own. "Steven, I love you, too. I really do."

Her declaration gave him the courage he needed.

Pulling out the small ring box, Steven opened it to reveal a pear-shaped diamond ring. "Will you do me the honor of becoming my wife?

Cherise could hardly comprehend what she'd just heard. *Had Steven actually proposed?* Gazing into his eyes, she found her answer. "Steven, are you sure about this? What do you think your parents will say?"

He chuckled. "We're not in high school, baby. I'm a grown man, Cherise. What

111

could they say?"

"I . . . I don't really know how to respond. I mean this is so incredible — it's so sweet and . . ." Cherise put her hand to her mouth, her eyes filling with tears.

"Honey, are you okay?"

She nodded. Removing her hand, she whispered, "I'm fine. This is so unexpected, Steven. This is so fast. I mean, this is *fast*."

"You said you loved me. You know that I love you. Baby, we love each other, and you know that we are right for each other. We fit, Cherise. We fit perfectly. Doesn't it feel right to you?"

She nodded, unable to speak.

"I'm going to ask you one more time," Steven said. "Will you marry me, Cherise Ransom?"

"Yes."

Steven blinked twice. "Did y-you just say yes?"

Tears sliding down her face, Cherise nodded. "Yes, I'll marry you."

Leaning over, Steven kissed her and placed the ring on her finger. "I love you, baby."

"If we do this, it has to be forever," Cherise said.

Steven agreed. "I want to spend my forever with you. You are the most perfect woman

I've ever met, and now you're going to be mine."

Later, while he slept, Cherise sat near the window in her room, playing with the ring on her finger.

He asked me to marry him. I'm getting married.

Cherise couldn't put into words the range of emotions running rampant through her right now. Steven had chosen her. He wanted to spend the rest of his life with her. This was huge.

Her happiness was marred later that evening when she watched the news. A gang of teens had burglarized and terrorized a poor family.

A sense of dread snaked down her spine. She didn't like hearing stuff like this — it always bothered her, and even now had put a damper on the excitement she'd felt earlier.

Cherise turned off the television.

She cast an anxious glance over at Steven, who lay on his side sleeping.

Will he still want to marry me when he discovers that I'm not as perfect as he seems to think?

CHAPTER 9

Maxie stood up and leaned over her desk to examine the ring more closely. "Oh my goodness! Girl, that's a rock if I ever saw one. I bet I can see that ring with my glasses off, and you know I'm almost as blind as a bat."

Cherise's grin spread from ear to ear. "It is nice, isn't it? But I don't really care about the size. Steven could have given me a cigar band, and I'd still marry him. He's such a sweetheart."

Maxie sat back down. "Well, congratulations, Cherise. You certainly deserve it."

"Thank you."

She called her mother.

"Mama, I have something to tell you," she began. "Last night Steven asked me to marry him. We're engaged."

"Oh my goodness! Congratulations, sweetie. I'm so happy for you. Amanda's told me that Steven is a really nice young man. I can't wait to meet him."

"I'm going to ask him to come to Phoenix with me soon," Cherise responded. "I want you to meet him."

"That would be wonderful," her mother exclaimed. "I can't wait to meet my future son-in-law."

"Now, Mama, I need you to keep this quiet. Steven and I are going to tell the clan on Sunday when we go out to Riverside for dinner. So don't say a word to Aunt Amanda."

"I won't. So have you set a wedding date yet?"

"Not yet." Cherise chuckled. "Steven just asked me last night."

They talked until she had to get off the phone to attend a meeting. Cherise was practically floating around the center. Everyone seemed to notice her glow and the ring on her left hand.

She gloried in their well wishes. Cherise felt totally fulfilled and complete. She was the person she had always longed to be and now everything was working out for her.

Cherise felt that she could finally lay her past to rest.

This time there would be no looking back.

Steven pulled into the parking lot of Rogers'

Florist. Sliding from under the wheel of his black Chrysler 300, he strolled happily into the shop, whistling a soft tune. Acknowledging the owner, he asked, "How're you doing, Mr. Rogers?"

"I'm doing fine, son. What can I do you for?"

"My girlfriend and I just got engaged. I want to get her something special."

"What? Did I hear you correctly?"

Nodding, Steven laughed. "You heard me right. I'm getting married."

The old man moved around the store gathering ribbons, roses and baby's breath. "Y'all remind me of me and Lizzie. I saw her come into church one Sunday shortly after she and her family moved here. I went over to her and introduced myself. I proposed to her seven days later. We just celebrated our fortieth wedding anniversary. We've had some good years . . ."

Steven shook his head, his eyes full of amusement as he listened to the gray-haired man talk while he worked.

When Mr. Rogers was done, he presented the bouquet of roses to Steven. "Well, what you think? Think she'll like it?"

Steven shook his head an emphatic yes. "I know she will. Cherise loves roses. Thanks, Mr. Rogers."

"Make sure I get my invitation to the wedding."

He chuckled. "I sure will, Mr. Rogers." Picking up the flowers, Steven strolled toward the door, stopping just in front of the entrance. "I'll even hand deliver it myself. Besides, I'm sure you'll be handling all of our floral needs."

Mr. Rogers laughed. "That'll be just fine. I'll see you, Steven. Tell your parents I said hello, will you?"

"I will. Thanks again."

Steven carefully placed the flowers in the seat on the passenger side. He climbed into the car and headed to Cherise's house.

One day in the near future, he would be driving home to her. *Home to Cherise.*

Thirty-five minutes later, Steven pulled into the driveway and parked his car.

He got out and strolled up the steps to the porch.

Whistling to himself, Steven rang the doorbell.

Cherise answered almost immediately, causing him to wonder if she'd been standing there waiting for him to arrive.

When he entered the house, the aroma of steaming seafood wafted to his nostrils.

Steven planted a kiss on her full lips and handed her the flowers. "Honey, I'm home," he announced.

"I'm glad," she said with a laugh.

He grinned. "You missed me?"

"Of course." She pointed toward the stairs. "I'm almost done with dinner. I have a surprise for you upstairs, so why don't you take a shower and get comfortable?" Cherise headed to the door that led into the kitchen.

Bending his head, Steven planted another wet kiss on her cheek. "I'll be back in a few minutes."

"I'm counting on it." Cherise smiled as she watched the man of her dreams make his way up the stairs. His muscular build tantalized her, causing her pulse to skitter alarmingly.

Cherise had dinner on the table by the time Steven returned, freshly showered and changed into the pair of silk pajamas she had laid out for him. In the soft candlelight, his bald head gleamed. His smooth, dark chestnut skin felt like satin to her touch. His strong African features held a certain sensuality.

Tall, dark and handsome, Steven made her feel loved. He had a way of making her feel like the most beautiful woman in the world.

As he neared, Cherise rushed into his arms. "I forgot to say thanks for my flowers earlier. They're lovely."

He kissed her passionately.

Cherise reluctantly pulled away. "We'd better eat before the food get cold."

He nodded. "I guess you're right. We can always pick up where we left off. Or we can have dinner for dessert." He smiled wickedly.

Her eyes wide and innocent, she asked, "But what would you have for dinner?"

"You."

Grinning, Cherise slowly untied her robe, displaying a beautiful silk teddy. Hearing Steven's sigh of pleasure gave her the confidence she needed.

Taking it off in a seductive manner, Cherise let it trail behind her as she led the way to her bedroom.

Upstairs, Steven traced a trail of scalding kisses along her pulsing throat while his hand set out on a journey of intimate discovery. In his eyes, Cherise could read the promise of delicious magic. She struggled to draw a breath, but she couldn't without inhaling his masculine fragrance. She felt the fire spreading through every fiber of her being until fervent desire pounded in rhythm with her thundering heart.

Steven's lips traveled to her breasts, causing fierce, restive feelings to uncoil inside her. Cherise was aching all over, shamelessly arching toward his moist lips and seeking hands, begging for more.

Obsessed with the feel of each other's hands and lips, the two fell back on the bed. Cherise's arms slid over Steven's sinewy shoulders to hold him close.

Passion streamed through Cherise like a river, sweeping her into a whirlpool of inexpressible splendor. The ever-changing, ever-growing sensations consumed her mind, body and soul.

Their energy spent, Steven and Cherise lay entwined. Feeling more content than she had ever felt in her life, Cherise smiled tenderly.

Gazing into her eyes, Steven kissed her softly. "You are my life, Cherise. I don't know what I'd do if I ever lost you."

"I'll never leave you. You've shown me what it's like to be completely loved. There's nothing or no one who could ever make me abandon what I have with you." And Cherise meant it with her entire being.

They showered together, then dressed in robes and went downstairs to reheat their dinner.

Later, Cherise dipped her lobster into the melted butter. "Mmm, this is good. It came out better than I thought."

Steven nodded. "You really outdid yourself tonight."

Grinning wickedly, Cherise asked, "In the kitchen or in the bedroom?"

"Both."

Her appetite for him was insatiable, and her lusty state of mind made Cherise weak with desire. Her breathing quickened at the sight of him licking his full, sexy lips.

Cherise had to mentally shake herself in order to concentrate on her dinner.

Setting his champagne flute on the table, Steven stated, "I guess we should decide on a wedding date."

She reached out across the table, lacing his fingers with her own. "I don't think we should rush it, but I don't know if I want to wait a whole year to marry you."

"I was thinking we could get married sometime in June," Steven tossed out in the conversation.

She frowned in discouragement, her delicate brow furrowing up. "That's about eight months away. I was thinking more of a spring wedding."

Steven shrugged. "Just think how warm and sunny it'll be . . . a perfect summer wedding outdoors. Now we just have to decide on a date."

Letting his hand go, Cherise said, "Okay, I'm convinced. June it is. We can do the date another night. We have more urgent things to deal with right now."

Pushing away from the table, Steven stood up.

Walking around the table to where Cherise sat, he pulled her to her feet. "You're right. For this moment, I just want to hold you."

She snuggled closer, whispering, "I love you so much, Steven. You're the best thing that's ever happened to me. I want you to know that. Sometimes I can't believe you are really a part of my life."

Steven's fingers curved under her chin, forcing her to look him in the eye. "I'm here for all of our lifetime."

Her heart sang with delight. Burying her face against the corded muscles of his chest, Cherise murmured, "What I'm feeling is so extraordinary, it defies description."

Running his fingers through her hair, Steven asked, "Now why is that?"

"Well, I have this incredible man that I love with all of my heart and who loves me back."

Suddenly feeling shy, Cherise pulled away from him and picked up a plate. "I know you probably think I'm being silly."

"No, I don't, because I feel the same way,

honey. I think anyone who's ever truly been in love knows what we're talking about. True love is a rare and precious find," Steven explained as he helped her clear the table.

He carried the last of the plates into the kitchen. "Hey, did I tell you that my aunt and uncle are moving back here? You're going to get to meet them real soon."

Putting the dishes into the dishwasher, Cherise replied, "That's great. I'm looking forward to it. You talk about them so much."

"I'm looking forward to seeing Aunt Eula Me. I haven't seen her since I went to Ghana to visit her." He frowned. "That was almost three years ago."

Cherise sighed. "From all you've told me about her, it's amazing she never had kids of her own."

His expression somber, Steven said, "That's because she can't have any. She was pregnant years ago, but the baby died in utero. She was fairly close to her due date."

Cherise swallowed hard. "Ooh, how terrible. I'm sorry to hear that."

Steven shook his head sadly. "Aunt Eula Mae never really got over losing that baby. I guess she just kind of transferred all her love to me."

"I don't know if anyone ever really gets

over something like that," Cherise said. "Losing a baby like that. I imagine something like that is hard to recover from."

"Yeah, it was hard on Aunt Eula. Real hard." Putting his arm around her, Steven said huskily, "Enough talking. Let's go up to bed."

Cherise couldn't agree more.

CHAPTER 10

"Miss Ransom, do you need help with anything?" Bridgett asked from the doorway. "Mrs. Sheppard said that you might need me to do something for you."

Cherise smiled, motioning for the teen to enter. Peering around the room once more, she nodded. "Actually, I really could use some help. Do you mind?"

"Naw," she responded. "I'll be glad to help you for a change."

"That's so sweet, Bridgett." Cherise sat forward in her chair, pointing to a stack of empty boxes. "Would you please return those to receiving?"

"Sure." She lifted the stack of cardboard boxes and headed to the door. "I'll be right back."

"Thanks, Bridgett. When you get back, I'd like for you to help me organize the file cabinet."

"No problem."

125

Bridgett returned promptly and the two of them spent the afternoon putting away the rest of the files.

Satisfied with the progress they'd made, Cherise commented, "You've been such a great help, Bridgett." She checked her watch. "It's getting late and I'm starving. How about I take you to lunch?"

Bridgett giggled. "You don't have to do that, Miss Ransom."

"I insist. It's my way of saying thanks for all of your hard work." Cherise gestured around the room. "I wouldn't have had any of this done without you."

Bridgett bobbed her head up and down. "Okay, we'll have lunch."

"We'll go wherever you want." Cherise picked up the phone. "I'm going to call Mrs. Sheppard and clear it with her."

Bridgett nodded as she continued putting away the last of the folders.

". . . Thanks, Maxie. Bye." Hanging up, Cherise asked, "Ready?"

"Ready." Bridgett completed the last of her filing. "I was thinking I'd like to go to K. C. Cagney & Company. It's not too far from here. About a mile south of Kendall Drive."

"Then that's where we'll go," Cherise agreed as she grabbed her purse.

She drove the short distance to the restaurant, twisting her face at the sight of the love bugs flying straight toward her car and smearing the windshields. Disgusted by the sight of the sticky bugs, Cherise made a mental note to stop off at a car wash after work.

She parked her car and they got out. Inside the restaurant, Cherise surveyed the campy fiftyish design, she commented, "I've never been here before. How is the food?"

"This is my favorite restaurant. My dad used to bring me here a lot . . ." Bridgett's voice drifted. "The food's real good." Her eyes became dark and desolate.

After they were seated, Cherise stated, "You don't talk about your father much. Is he still alive?"

"Just my mother's dead. I used to live with my dad." Shrugging, Bridgett added, "I guess I never really talk about him 'cause there's not much to say about him. Except that he used to love me and now he doesn't."

A glint of wonder in her eyes, Cherise asked softly, "You don't really believe that, do you?"

Bridgett suddenly seemed wistful. "I do. See, he loved me until he got married again. He has a new family now and there's no room for me in it."

"Just because he's remarried, it doesn't mean he's stopped loving you."

"My dad had to make a choice. He chose them."

Cherise frowned. "I'm afraid I don't understand."

"It's simple, Miss Ransom. His wife made him choose between them and me. They won," Bridgett stated bitterly.

"Who would tell you something like that?" Cherise asked, wanting to put all the pieces together. She was sure that Bridgett was maybe feeling a little jealous, and that was normal. For years it had been just the two of them.

"I know what you're thinking and you're wrong. Nobody had to tell me anything." She pointed to herself. "I heard them talking myself. His old skinny wife told him that he had to choose between them and his pig of a daughter." Bridgett's eyes filled with unshed tears. "Well, guess what? His fat daughter lost out."

Cherise reached over to cover Bridgett's trembling hand. "I'm so sorry."

"You know, Miss Ransom, what really hurts is that he let her call me names like that and he never got mad. Sometimes he would laugh with her and her daughter."

Bridgett paused as if summoning the courage to continue.

"I overheard the witch tell him that she wouldn't have sex with him again until after I was out of the house. You should've seen him. He hurried up and he sent me to my grandmother." Sighing, she murmured, "I guess I didn't deserve a mother or a father. My mom dying when I was a baby and my dad . . ."

Fighting back her own tears of anger, Cherise squeezed Bridgett's hand. "Your father doesn't deserve a daughter like you. But you know what? I have a strong feeling that one day you'll look up and he's going to be there. I truly believe that."

"I still love him, you know," she whispered. "I don't want to talk to him or anything 'cause I'm still angry and my feelings are hurt. But even after all he's done, I still love him."

"When you're ready to talk to him, you will."

Shrugging, Bridgett stated, "Maybe. Maybe not." Picking up her menu, she said, "I think I'll have a turkey burger."

Cherise smiled. "I think that sounds wonderful. I'll have the same."

She gasped in surprise when she returned

to find a huge bouquet of flowers in her office.

Reading the card, she smiled. They were from the staff to congratulate her on her engagement.

Steven called and she told him about the flowers.

"It's always nice to be appreciated." She didn't respond, so he asked, "Honey, what's going on? You sound as if you need something to brighten your day."

She sat on the corner of her desk. "I just had lunch with one of the teens here. Steven, she's so sweet and the poor thing's been through so much."

"She's not alone, honey. She has you." His tone was soothing.

"I know. I just hope she'll continue making progress. When she first came here, she was so angry and she wouldn't open up to anyone. But each day she reveals more and more about herself."

"Sounds to me like you're reaching her."

"I hope so," she murmured almost to herself.

"Are you afraid of a setback of some kind?" Steven asked.

Her face clouded with uneasiness. "I don't really know. I just want something good to happen to her. She should be enjoying her youth."

Something I missed out on, Cherise added silently.

"You really care about her, don't you?"

"Steven, I care about all of the children here. I worry about them all."

"I'm glad they have you. Hell, I'm glad I have you. You are one special lady."

Cherise grinned. "I bet you say that to all of your girlfriends," she teased.

"Just the top three. Honey, I've got to get to a meeting. I called to let you know I was thinking about you. I'll see you later at your place."

"Okay," Cherise responded. "Oh, I'm going to stop by the mall. I need to pick up some things before I head home."

"Remember we're going house hunting and we still have a wedding and honeymoon to pay for."

She smiled. "Don't worry, I haven't forgotten. See you."

Cherise hung up.

Leaning over, she inhaled the sweet fragrance of the flowers once more before getting back to work. The roses from Steven still sat on her desk, so she moved these to the credenza near the window.

That evening Cherise arrived home laden

with shopping bags.

She put them in her bedroom, then checked her answering machine for messages.

Steven had called earlier and stated he was still at the office but would be leaving in the next half hour.

Navigating to the den, she kicked off her shoes in a carefree manner before dropping down on the sofa. Cherise reached for the remote control and began surfing the channels.

Although Cherise missed Steven, she was delighted to have this time to herself. Since he probably wouldn't be there for another hour, she didn't have to worry about rushing dinner.

Closing her eyes, Cherise tried to relax.

She couldn't get Bridgett off of her mind.

Steven leaned back into the comfort of his chair, staring at a photo of Cherise. He was excited over the fact that she would soon meet his aunt and uncle. They were the two people who meant as much to him as his parents.

Aunt Eula Mae was a strong-willed, outspoken woman, and he was relieved that she was readily prepared to accept Cherise — a rare quality in her. As long as he could remember, she'd never taken a liking to anybody he'd dated. Always found something wrong with them.

Smiling, Steven had to admit that his aunt had always been right in her feelings. But this time was different. Steven had a feeling Aunt Eula Mae and Cherise would instantly hit it off.

Cherise was his soul mate — he'd known that from the first moment he'd laid eyes on her. His aunt would see it, too.

Aunt Eula Mae. He couldn't wait to see her again.

Grinning, Steven cut off his monitor.

It was getting late and he wanted to get to Cherise's place. His heart still performed somersaults whenever he thought of her. It was obvious to everyone that he loved her to no end.

Steven gave thanks that Aunt Eula Mae was willing enough to give Cherise the benefit of the doubt. If she disliked a person she would have nothing to do with them. That could make for a tense situation, leaving him to choose sides. Steven didn't want to be a part of something like that.

Standing up, he assured himself that there was nothing to worry about.

Aunt Eula Mae would come to love Cherise as much as he did.

CHAPTER 11

Cherise opened the door to let her sister enter. She and Jazz were going to have a girl's day. Since she'd started seeing Steven, they hadn't spent much time together.

"Jazz, come on in. I've got some stuff to tell you!" She admired the cute little one-button wrap skirt in denim that her sister was wearing. "Make yourself comfortable and I'll get the coffee."

Jazz strolled into the living room and plopped down on the floral-patterned love seat. Glancing around the room, she asked, "Where's Steven? I thought for sure I'd see his car parked in the driveway."

Cherise walked in and handed a cup of flavored coffee to Jazz before sitting down beside her. "For your information he was here, but he's gone to the gym and then he's hanging with some of his boys." She blew softly on the steaming hot coffee.

Jazz giggled. "Are you two tired of each

other already?"

"Of course not," Cherise responded and held up her left hand.

Jazz's eyes widened, then filled with tears of happiness. "Oh, Lord! That sure is a beauty." She hugged Cherise, causing her to almost spill the contents of her cup. "I'm so happy for you."

Cherise placed her cup and saucer on the coffee table and said, "Steven and I are going to make an announcement tomorrow at Aunt Amanda's house. Don't say anything before then, okay?"

"I'm not saying a word. Have you two set a wedding date?" Pressing her hand to her bosom, Jazz asked, "I am the maid of honor, right?"

Cherise laughed. "We've decided on the month, but not the date. Probably late June. And *yes,* you're going to be my maid of honor."

Jazz chewed her lower lip petulantly before she responded, "I'm just a little bit jealous. I wish I had someone in my life who loved me as much as Steven loves you."

Deep down, she wished that same for her sister. She wanted Jazz to find the same happiness she'd found with Steven.

"Cherise, can I ask you something?"

"Sure. What's up?"

"Why did you leave home?" Jazz asked. "Were you mad with Mama? Did you two have a fight or something?"

Her sister had never asked her about this — neither had her brothers. When she'd left home, Jazz had been thirteen years old.

"Mom and I didn't have a fight," Cherise responded. "It wasn't like I wanted to leave you guys behind, but I hated school. You have no idea how those kids used to treat me. I was picked on all the time and called fat, a pig, even an elephant once."

Jazz was shocked. "I had no idea."

"Nobody really did because I never told anyone. I thought if I didn't acknowledge it they would just stop."

"You used to run with these two girls," Jazz said. "Tina Smith and Joyce Sanders."

Just the sound of their names brought back a rush of unpleasant memories. Tina and Joyce were part of the pretty and popular clique, but they were also bad news, although Cherise didn't know it at the time. All she wanted was to have them as friends.

"Tina ended up going to prison for identity fraud," Jazz announced.

This time Cherise was surprised by the news. "Are you serious? How did you find out?"

"I was home visiting Mama last summer

and it was all over the news. I meant to tell you, but I kept forgetting about it."

Deep down she wasn't surprised that Tina had ended up in prison. She had been shoplifting since high school. Joyce was right along with her. Cherise had desperately wanted them to like her, so she attempted to buy their friendship by stealing money from her mother's purse and giving it to them. Soon that was not enough. They demanded more for their friendship.

"I asked Cherise to marry me and she said yes," Steven announced after dinner and before dessert was served at Aunt Amanda's house. Most of the Ransoms were there, except for Prescott and his family, but only because they lived out of state.

Ivy jumped up to hug the happy couple.

Congratulations and well wishes rang out from around the dining room.

"You never said a word," Elle accused. "I talked to you twice this week. How long have you two been engaged?"

"Just a few days," Cherise responded. "We wanted to wait and tell everyone together."

Amanda brought out a bottle of champagne for the adults and sparkling cider for the children.

Steven kissed her.

After their mini celebration in Riverside, they drove back to Los Angeles. Once they were at his place, Steven called his aunt to share their news.

"Aunt Eula Mae, how're you doing?" He inquired upon hearing her pick up.

Cherise couldn't hear what she was saying, but whatever it was, it made him laugh.

"That's fine, Aunt Eula Mae. I'm calling to tell you my news." He paused for effect. "Remember the woman I've been telling you about? Well, I asked Cherise to marry me and she said yes."

Cherise didn't realize that she had been holding her breath until Steven said, "I knew that you'd be happy for me. Now when are you moving back to the States?"

A big smile spread over his face.

"What?" Cherise whispered.

"They will be here in a couple of weeks," he mouthed.

"That's great. I can't wait to see you, Aunt Eula Mae," Steven said. "And Uncle Jerome. I've missed you both so much. Cherise is looking forward to meeting you. By the way, she told me to tell you hello."

He winked at Cherise. "You're going to love her."

Steven spoke with his uncle for a few minutes before hanging up and giving

Cherise all his attention.

She felt Steven's hard, lean body trying to stretch out beside her on the overstuffed sofa. She chuckled. "Now, you know that you can't lie down on this couch with me. Let me sit up, then we'll both be comfortable."

His large hand took her face and held it gently. "I have a much better idea. Why don't we just go lie down on the bed? I know we'll be comfortable in there."

"You know you have a one-track mind, Steven. All you think about is sex," she teased.

Steven's eyes roamed over her full figure, caressing her softness. "Well, I've got this sexy woman here, looking all good all the time. What else do you expect me to think about? Girl, you drive me crazy."

Her eyes caught and held his. "You're not just saying this to me, are you? Do you mean it?"

"Honey, you know how much you turn me on. You look so good to me, girl." His expression was one of lust.

Cherise grinned. "I guess I just wanted to hear you say it again and again."

"I know, sweetheart. But I'm not just saying it because I know you need to hear it —

I'm saying it because it's the way I really feel."

Cherise smiled, her heart full of love. "How did I get to be so lucky?"

"I'm the lucky one, sweetheart. You're exactly the woman I was looking for. I knew it the very first moment I saw you. Standing at the elevator in that black outfit —"

She cut him off by asking, "You remember what I was wearing the day we met on the ship?" She was touched by his revelation.

"Yeah, it's a day I'll never forget. I have always wanted a woman who was just as beautiful on the inside as the outside. I love the way you carry yourself and the way you're always going after what you want. We're kindred spirits, you and I."

She laid her head in the crook of his neck, contented. "You make me feel special, Steven."

"That's because you are," he responded.

Cherise lifted her lips to his.

Steven kissed her mouth in a tender brushing of his lips that made her smile.

Steven and Cherise flew to Phoenix the following weekend.

It was time for her mother to meet the man she planned to marry in June. They had finally decided to do it the last Saturday in the month.

"Our offer on the house was accepted, and they'll start building in about a month," Cherise told her mother while they were at the dining room table going over bridal magazines. Steven was out with her oldest brother picking up snacks for the football game coming on later that afternoon.

"I'm so excited, and I know once you see the house, you're going to love it."

"Is it going to be ready by the time you get married?"

"It should be almost done. I'm selling my house, and after we get married we'll be staying in Steven's house. His aunt and uncle are going to move into Steven's house after we move into the new house."

Arlene broke into a grin. "I really like him. You did good."

Cherise closed her eyes, but tears escaped, rolling down her cheeks. "I can't believe I'm this happy, Mama. I love Steven so much. Sometimes I feel like I don't really deserve him."

Smiling, Arlene handed her a tissue. "Honey, you deserve it. Now, no more crying. We've got a wedding to plan."

Dabbing at her eyes, Cherise nodded. Things were perfect between her and Steven, and she wanted to keep it that way.

CHAPTER 12

On Thanksgiving Day, Cherise opened the door to Steven's house, and her senses were immediately assaulted by the smell of scented candles.

"Steven?" she called out. "Steven, where are you?"

"I'm in the bedroom, honey," he yelled back. "I'll be right down."

Putting her purse down on a nearby table, she stood in the middle of the living room, glancing around, taking in everything.

Flickering gold candles were placed everywhere, providing the room's only source of light. Soft jazz flowed in the background.

Smiling, Cherise took off her black single-breasted jacket, laying it neatly across the back of the sofa. She basked in the romantic ambience, whispering, "What are you up to?"

Steven eased up behind her, wrapping his arms around her waist. "Happy Thanksgiving, sweetheart," he said. "Did you have fun with your family?"

"It was good, but I'm glad to be here with you." Cherise turned around in his embrace, burying her face against his throat. "This wasn't the way I wanted to spend our first Thanksgiving."

"I know, but since my mom wasn't feeling well, I figured I'd cook for them. You were on my mind all day long." He spoke with a huskiness that indicated his hunger for her.

Peering up at him, Cherise inquired, "What's with all the candles and the soft music? What exactly have you planned?"

"What do you think? I'm seducing you," he whispered, his breath hot against her ear.

Leaning into his embrace, she said, "Mmm, I like the sound of that."

With one hand, he pulled her closer to him.

Cherise closed her eyes to the feel of his smooth, handsome face against hers. Steven kissed her, opening her mouth with his.

He pulled away from her, leaving her hungry for more of his kisses. "I have a surprise for you."

"You're spoiling me, Steven."

"You deserve to be spoiled, sweetheart. I love spoiling you." He walked across the room to pick up a large manila envelope.

"Here." Steven handed it to her.

Cherise opened it and read the contents. Her mouth opened in astonishment. "You named a star after me?"

Steven nodded and smiled. "Yes, I did. Would you like to see your star?"

"Yes." Like an eager child, Cherise followed him to the patio, where he had a telescope already sat up.

"Come here, sweetheart. Look at this."

Peering through the tiny hole, she asked excitedly, "Is that it? Is that my star?"

"It sure is."

She turned around, facing him. "Thank you so much. I can't tell you how much this means to me —"

"Shh, just kiss me." Steven demanded. His kiss sent new spirals of ecstasy through her. Moving gently down the length of her back, his hands caused Cherise to gasp in sweet agony. She wrapped her arms around him, pulling him close.

The feel of his firm, muscled flesh was intoxicating and she felt the golden wave of passion and love that flowed between them.

"I guess we should go back inside," Steven suggested.

Cherise shook her head no. "Let's eat out here. It's such a beautiful night; I just want to enjoy it."

He nodded. "Anything you want, honey."

Steven stepped inside the house. Cherise followed him, helping him carry the dinner and a bottle of chilled wine.

Wiping her mouth with her napkin, she said, "This is so romantic, Steven. We should do this more often."

He laughed and pointed his fork toward her. "You're not going to get out of cooking. I know you."

She joined in his laughter. "Well, you can't blame a girl for trying. Seriously though, I've enjoyed everything."

"I'm glad." Steven glanced up into the night. "It was a good idea to come out here to eat."

Cherise pushed away from the table. "Why don't we go inside and work off some of this food?" Recognizing the lusty look in Steven's eyes, she added, "Dancing, honey. I'm just talking about dancing."

"That's just what I was thinking," he replied in mock innocence.

Cherise burst into laughter. "Oh yeah, I really believe that."

They headed inside, holding hands. Steven led her to the middle of the living room floor. Pushing the huge coffee table to the side, he created the illusion of a dance floor.

"I guess great minds do think alike,

because I have a gift for you, too." Cherise walked over to a nearby table and pulled a small box from her purse.

Cherise had purchased a pair of platinum architect-triangle cuff links, which Steven seemed to love. "I saw them in the store and knew that I had to get them for you."

"These are great," he told her. "Thanks, baby. How would you feel about spending Christmas in Jamaica?"

She smiled. "It sounds like fun. Why?"

Steven presented her with tickets to Jamaica.

"Are you serious?" she asked.

He nodded. "I want our first Christmas together to be special."

"I'm so looking forward to the trip," Cherise told him. "This has been the best Thanksgiving ever."

He smiled. "I feel the same way."

Cherise and Steven held each other tightly as they danced to the romantic sounds of Luther Vandross, Brian McKnight and James Ingram. In the tightness of his embrace, Cherise felt safe and secure. As Steven sang to her, an easy smile hovered about her lips.

Tracing the perfectly shaped star on her shoulder, he murmured, "You know I really love your birthmark. It's very sexy."

Cherise laughed. "Really?"

"I think so. That's what prompted me to buy you the star." He stared into her eyes. "I love you so much."

"I love you, too, Steven, with my entire being."

Together they savored the warmth of each other's bodies and the kindling of heated excitement. Tonight they were the only two people in the world.

Cherise's heart swelled with happiness as he held her tightly and their mouths joined. In Steven, she had found the peace she had been searching for.

Here in his arms, she would be content forever.

CHAPTER 13

Cherise and Steven had gotten up at the crack of dawn to open Christmas presents. He had given her a new iPod touch, a stunning sapphire-and-diamond tennis bracelet with matching earrings, and the designer handbag she'd wanted.

They burst into laughter when Steven opened his gift containing an iPod touch. Cherise also gave him a new leather briefcase and a couple of sweaters.

Steven called his family while Cherise was in the other room, talking to her sister. She called her mother next. She finished her call when Steven came to the door to let her know that their breakfast had arrived.

"I have an idea about our wedding theme," Cherise said as she buttered her toast.

Steven sat down his coffee cup, listening.

"Since we met on a cruise, I was thinking we could have a Mediterranean-themed wedding."

He nodded in approval. "I like that."

Cherise stuck a forkful of eggs in her mouth. She chewed and swallowed before saying, "I'll meet with Kaitlin when we get home. She's got some of the most beautiful wedding gowns in her shop."

When they finished eating, they got up and dressed for the beach.

"I'm so glad we decided to spend Christmas here in Jamaica," Cherise said as they walked out of their suite in the Grand Lido Hotel and down the hallway toward the elevator. "I could stay here forever."

Steven nodded. "I know what you mean. I love this island. This is only my second time coming here but it feels like a second home."

As soon as they stepped outside, Cherise drank in her surroundings. It was so amazing how the sunny weather just seemed to wash the island in brilliant waves of color. Yellows drenched by the sun, passionate pinks, delectable purples, tropical teals and opulent greens.

Immersed in the sea of heavenly hues as people milled around them, Steven and Cherise strolled casually along the sandy beach looking for a vacant area to place their belongings. They soon found a spot and spread their towels down before dropping down to the ground.

Surveying the Seven Mile Beach, Cherise admired its beauty. "I really needed this little getaway. Since my promotion, seems like I can't keep my desk clear."

Steven agreed.

They spent time swimming in the ocean, then decided to take another walk.

He held her hand and kept her close to him at all times, which thrilled Cherise. No man had ever made her feel so special.

"What are you thinking about?" Steven asked, intruding on her thoughts.

"I was just thinking that no man I've ever dated has made me feel the way you do. You treat me like a queen."

"That's because you are a queen to me," Steven interjected. "A woman who is as beautiful on the inside as you are on the outside deserves to be treated like royalty. I love and appreciate your friendship, your love and your honesty."

Cherise stiffened a little when he mentioned the word honesty. She had been as honest as she could with him.

Cherise cleared her throat nervously. "I'm not perfect, Steven. I do have flaws."

He met her gaze. "You are perfect in every way to me."

Cherise didn't respond.

■ ■ ■ ■

When she returned from Jamaica five days later, Cherise met up with her cousins Kaitlin and Elle for a spa date.

"Now, you know the rules," Kaitlin said. "You were supposed to take me and Matt with you."

"Uh-huh." Cherise laughed. "Girl, we were trying to get away from the clan for a few days."

"Did you have fun?" Elle asked.

"We did. We spent most of our time on the beach. Steven and I both love the water. That's why we're building the house in Santa Monica, so that we'll be near the water all the time."

"That's so sweet," Kaitlin said. "Matt and I have been looking in that area too."

Elle's head popped up from the magazine she was reading. "You guys are selling your house?"

"We haven't put it on the market yet, but yeah. Matt wants a bigger house and he loves the water, too."

"Brennen would probably like something bigger, but I'm perfectly happy where I am." Elle checked her vibrating cell phone. "That's him calling now."

Cherise grinned. "I can't wait to get married."

"You should be. I love being married to Matt. He's a wonderful husband and father."

"I think Steven is going to be a great father. We've been talking about starting a family right away. I made a doctor's appointment to check out everything. I want to make sure I'm in working order, you know?"

Kaitlin laughed. "You are too funny."

Cherise grew serious. "Steven is always talking about how perfect I am — I worry that he's going to be disappointed when he starts to see all my flaws."

"Honey, he knows that you're not perfect — nobody is. But even with your imperfections, you still seem perfect to him. That's what he's saying," Kaitlin explained.

"That's what I'm hoping," Cherise said. "I don't like all the references to perfection. I don't need the pressure."

Kaitlin smiled. "Well, the way I see it, we are perfect. Just ask any of the men in our lives."

Cherise picked up a bridal magazine and said, "Oh, we want a Mediterranean-themed wedding."

"That sounds wonderful," Elle interjected.

152

"We can even do that for your bridal shower as well. We can send out the invitation on postcards from Italy, Greece and France. Ask the guests to bring a gift with a Mediterranean theme such as French lingerie or maybe a cookbook from one of the countries."

Kaitlin nodded in agreement. "I like that."

"So do I," Cherise said with a grin. "We could have that drink from Spain — I forgot the name, but it's made with red wine and lemonade."

"Oh, it's Tinto de Verano," Kaitlin said.

"You can give out gift bags with French chocolates or soaps for shower favors," Elle suggested.

"Or half bottles of Spanish or Italian wines," Kaitlin contributed. "But then, not everyone drinks."

"Sparkling water is a favorite all over the Mediterranean," Cherise said. "We could give out some in the gift bags. I could have a special thank-you note printed on the label."

"So what colors are you thinking of using for the wedding?" Kaitlin asked.

"I'm thinking rich olive green and gold. And for the wedding reception, I think those colors should be infused with brilliant blues throughout the room, with wine-colored candles." Cherise gave a slight shrug. "At least this is what's at the top of my head."

"Well, we have time to sort everything out," Kaitlin assured her. "I'm so happy for you, Cherise. You're getting married."

"I know. I still have to pinch myself to make sure I'm not dreaming."

It was time for them to have their facials, so they tabled their discussion until later.

Steven and Cherise attended church service with the rest of the clan on Sunday. Cherise wore a navy-and-white dress with matching accessories, while Steven looked handsome in a navy suit.

Cherise felt beautiful.

After church, they all headed to Amanda's house for a traditional clan gathering.

Cherise had already dropped off the cake she and Steven had baked before church. Steven's parents were going to be joining them for dinner so that they could meet everyone.

She made a quick call to her mother.

"You all made it," she heard Steven say, and knew that his parents had arrived.

Cherise made her way through the dining room.

She and Rebecca Chambers embraced. "It's so good to see you, dear."

"It's good to see you too," Cherise replied.

Amanda and Rebecca hit it off immediately.

Dinner was served thirty minutes later.

Cherise leaned over toward Steven and said, "Your parents are fitting in nicely."

"Remember, my mom comes from a large family, so she's used to this."

Steven's father was in conversation with William Ragland when Cherise caught the expression on Ivy's face. She was still not thrilled with the idea of her mother having male companionship. From the look on Ray's face, he wasn't either.

Cherise's expression changed when her father walked in with a woman who looked young enough to be his daughter.

Jazz glanced over at her and the two exchanged puzzled looks.

He introduced her as his friend from North Carolina and said her name was Laura.

Cherise noticed that her brother Julian didn't even acknowledge their father. Instead, he excused himself from the table and headed outside to the patio. Laine waited a moment before getting up to follow him.

"Is Julian okay?" Steven asked.

She nodded. "He has some abandonment issues with my father, but he's fine."

Despite the tense moments, the clan had a wonderful dinner and afterward gathered outside for a basket ball game.

Cherise sat down with the women to cheer on their men.

Jazz was the only girl playing and was on Matt's team along with Steven and Ransom.

"Your sister can ball," Steven said when he sat down beside her. "I see why she's coaching the basketball team for Long Beach University."

"She's been approached by the Los Angeles Larks to coach their team."

Steven's eyes rose in surprise. "Really?"

"She's had two interviews and I'm pretty sure she might be joining the coaching staff."

"That's great," he said.

"Her team has gone undefeated for the two years that she's been on staff and she's the youngest head coach for a university in history, but then she graduated high school when she was sixteen and received a full ride from USC for basketball."

They headed back to Los Angeles shortly after seven with his parents following behind in their car.

"My mom and dad really enjoyed themselves today," Steven said.

"How about you? Did you have a good time?"

He gave her a sidelong glance. "I always have a great time with your family. It's good that we all get along."

"I hope when your aunt comes home that we'll be friends. I know how much she means to you, Steven. I don't want to come between that."

He reached over and took her hand in his. "You don't have anything to worry about. Aunt Eula Mae is one of the most caring women you will ever meet. She isn't wishy-washy with her feelings either. She will either love you or dislike you — there is no in-between with her."

CHAPTER 14

Steven let himself into Cherise's town house with the set of keys she'd given him. "Honey, are you here?" He called out.

"I'm in here."

He strolled through the dining room en route to the den, following the sound of her voice.

She was sitting in the middle of her floor making notes in several folders. Steven knew she was updating her case files.

He planted a kiss on Cherise's cheek. "Hey, baby. How was your day?"

"Great," she murmured. "It was a good day. All of my girls were well-behaved and responsive during group this afternoon. I'm so proud of them."

He sat down on the sofa not too far from where she was sitting. "I have some wonderful news. Aunt Eula Mae and Uncle Jerome are here."

Cherise broke into a grin. "That's wonderful. I know how much you've been looking forward to seeing them."

Steven stood up and walked over to the pantry in search of something to snack on. "They came in last night. I can't wait to see them. My mom wants us to come over for dinner tomorrow night. It's kind of a family celebration for Aunt Eula Mae and Uncle Jerome."

Cherise looked up at him. "You're really excited, aren't you? Your aunt really is the light of your life."

She folded her arms across her chest, then said, "Maybe I should be jealous . . ."

Grinning, Steven shook his head. "Sweetheart, you have nothing to worry about. Yeah, I love my Aunt Eula Mae, but you — you are my lady. You are the light of my life."

With long, purposeful strides, Steven made his way to the refrigerator and retrieved an apple. He bit into it, chewing thoughtfully, "You're sure you don't mind? I know this is sort of last-minute —"

Her arms folded across her ample bosom, Cherise inclined her head. "Now, why should I mind, Steven? I know how much you want to see your aunt and uncle. I'm not that selfish, you know."

Cherise prayed deep down that she and Eula Mae Stewart would become the best of friends. Steven was so close to his aunt that if she and Eula Mae didn't get along, it could have a strong effect on their marriage.

Her family was very accepting of others, so there was hardly ever drama when it came to choosing mates. She had no desire to be placed in the middle of Steven and his aunt.

Now, Steven was getting on Cherise's last nerve.

One would think they were about to have dinner with the President of the United States by the way he was acting. It was just his aunt and uncle. This dinner was supposed to be drama-free.

He checked his watch a third time and said. "Honey, if you don't hurry up, we're going to be late for dinner. You know traffic's crazy this time of day."

On the floor, Cherise scrambled around the bed, looking under it. "I'm looking for my shoes. I don't see them anywhere."

"I told you that you have too many pairs anyway," he huffed.

Cherise tried to keep her frustration at bay. "Steven, you're not helping me by complaining. Why don't you try helping me instead?"

"Which ones are you looking for?"

"The black ones."

Steven walked over to the closet and stepped inside. "And you have how many pairs of black shoes?"

Cherise sighed in her irritation. "Steven, the ones with the ankle strap."

Steven asked, "You mean the ones sitting under the chair in here?"

Still on all fours, Cherise peeked from the left side of the bed. "Yes, that's them. I don't remember putting them over there."

"You didn't. You asked me to get them for you right before you took your shower."

Cherise released a soft sigh. "Then why didn't you say that?"

"Honey, I thought you'd decided to wear another pair. Every time I've walked out of this room and come back, you have on something different." He chuckled. "You're nervous, aren't you?"

Standing up, Cherise gave an irritable tug at her sleeve. "It's not funny, Steven. I know it may sound stupid to you, but I really want to make a good impression on your aunt and uncle. I know how much they mean to you."

Leaning casually against the frame of the door, Steven's mouth curved into a smile. "I remember the day you met my parents. I thought I was going to have to unglue you from the car."

"These people are very important to you, Steven. I want them to like me. Surely you can understand why I was so nervous."

"My parents are crazy about you. Just like I said they would be. Aunt Eula Mae and Uncle Jerome will love you too. You wait and see."

"I hope so." Cherise grabbed her purse and headed out of the bedroom. "I'll settle for them just liking me."

"Stop worrying yourself, sweetheart. I know they will." He patted her on the behind.

Twenty minutes later, they arrived at a large brick house. It was the home Steven had grown up in. Cherise loved the older Georgian-style two-story house. She was excited to finally meet Eula Mae. She'd seen pictures of her in Steven's home and at his parents', but it was nice to finally meet her in person.

Steven opened the door, allowing her to walk in ahead of him. They were greeted by his mother.

"Hi, kids. I was just about to call over there to see what was taking so long for you to get here. Eula Mae's been dying to see you both."

Steven kissed his mother's cheek. "Hello,

Mama. How're you feeling these days?"

Rebecca gave Cherise a hug before responding. "I'm doing fine. I still tire kind of easy." She grinned. "But I suspect it's just old age creeping in."

"Are you taking vitamins?" Cherise asked.

Rebecca shook her head. "No, I haven't, but I've been thinking about getting me some. Some of those multivitamins."

Nodding, Cherise agreed. "I think you'll be able to see a difference in the way you're feeling if you start taking them."

"I'll get me some tomorrow. Come on, you two, everybody's in the den right now."

They followed her toward the back of the house. Steven immediately rushed over to embrace a slender woman of medium height. Cherise estimated her to be in her mid-forties. She smiled and moved closer.

"Aunt Eula Mae, Uncle Jerome. I have someone very special that I want you both to meet." Holding her hand, Steven pulled Cherise closer to him. "This is my fiancée, Cherise Ransom."

She opened her mouth to speak and almost choked on her words. "Mr. and Mrs. Stewart, it's so nice to finally meet you." Her heart was beating so fast, Cherise felt like the room was spinning.

Steven slipped an arm around her.

They settled down in the living room.

Cherise wasn't sure she'd ever seen Steven so happy. It was obvious that he loved his aunt as much as he loved his mother.

Rebecca announced that dinner was ready and they all got up and headed to the dining room.

"I told you that she was going to love you," Steven whispered in her ear.

Cherise relaxed, grateful that Eula Mae didn't hate her.

She enjoyed listening to Eula Mae and her husband discuss their lives in Ghana.

"I loved Ghana, but I'm so glad to be back home," Eula Mae said.

"I'm glad you didn't decide to move back to Phoenix," Rebecca said. "It's going to be nice to have you here in L.A."

"Cherise is from Phoenix as well," Steven announced.

She took a sip of her lemonade. "My mother is still there," Cherise said. "I left when I was fifteen to come here to L.A."

"We thought about moving back there, but Eula Mae didn't want to do it," Jerome stated. "She wants to be here in California."

Cherise caught a glimpse of sadness in Eula Mae's eyes and for a brief moment, it felt like déjà vu. It was as if she'd seen that look before, but she and Eula Mae had never met until now.

Seeing Steven and his family like this reminded her of the clan dinners. Cherise felt like once they were married, they would all be one big happy family, and the thought pleased her immensely.

Cherise offered to help with cleanup after dinner, but Rebecca turned her down.

She and Steven sat down in the family room with Eula Mae and Jerome.

They stayed until it was almost eleven o'clock.

Cherise yawned, prompting Steven to say, "I guess we need to call it a night. My baby and I have early days tomorrow."

He got up and hugged his aunt and uncle once more. "I'm so glad you're back."

Steven dropped Cherise off at her place before driving to his house.

"Honey, I'll see you tomorrow," he told her. "If I didn't have that breakfast meeting planned in the morning, I'd spend the night."

"I know, sweetie. I have a staff meeting at eight that I still need to prepare for." Cherise yawned again. She was tired.

As soon as she walked into her house, Cherise made her way upstairs and went straight to the shower. She was going to bed.

Last night she hadn't slept well over the

anticipation of meeting Eula Mae. The evening had gone well, and now the anxious anticipation she'd felt earlier had dissipated.

It was a dreary, dismal February first.

Dark gray thunderclouds rolled over Los Angeles and stretched out across the ocean, but they didn't put a damper on Cherise's feelings. She was deliriously happy, and nothing could change that.

She left her office after her group session to meet her sister and mother at the bridal shop. Arlene had flown in a couple of hours ago to help Cherise select a wedding gown.

A loud thunderous noise passed through the air, and the heavens seemed to tremble with anger as the rain came down harder. Running to her car, Cherise wondered if somehow the weather was a bad omen. She quickly shrugged off the thought. Things were great between her and Steven.

Completely drenched, she made it to her car and drove to the Bridal Boutique.

Her mother and Jazz were already there.

"Honey, I was about to get worried about you," Arlene said, wiping the water from Cherise's face. "I called you at work and they said you'd already left. I called your cell but didn't get an answer."

"I didn't hear my cell ring," she responded. "It took me longer to get here because of the weather. Is Kaitlin here?"

Jazz shook her head. "She had to leave because Travaile got sick at school. She's going to take her to Daisi and then she'll come back here."

A smiling sales associate walked over to them and said, "Are you ready, Miss Ransom? Kaitlin selected several gowns for you to try on. They're already in the dressing room."

Smiling, Cherise nodded.

She spent the next couple of hours trying on gown after gown. They were all beautiful, but none of them really spoke to her.

Jazz knocked on the door and announced, "Kaitlin's back."

Cherise held the last dress in front of her as she eyed her reflection. It had an Empire waist and featured a delicate chiffon overlay with a flyaway panel. Satin rosebuds in white with olive-green leaves adorned the front and back neckline.

Cherise put it on. When she stepped out of the room, the sales associate zipped her up.

"I love the way this one looks on me," she whispered.

"Steven is not going to believe that this exquisite woman floating down the aisle toward him is his soul mate. Cherise, you're beautiful, girl, but looking at you in this dress . . ." Jazz's eyes filled with tears. "There aren't any words to describe . . ." She accepted the tissue the associate handed her and wiped her face.

Cherise met her mother's gaze.

"This is the one," Arlene said. "It's perfect."

Joining them, Kaitlin agreed. "When this one arrived yesterday, I knew that it would be the one for you. Instead of a veil, I think you should have a satin ribbon woven through an upswept hairstyle. We can have rosebuds like the one on the gown sewn on the ribbon."

Cherise nodded in approval. "I've found my dress."

Kaitlin left for a moment, then returned carrying an olive green, Grecian-style dress. "What do you think of this for the bridesmaids? It's flattering on any figure. I have another one that's similar to this, except the bodice has gold beading across the front."

Cherise looked at her sister, who said, "I saw that one up front. I like it."

"I'll get it so that you can try it on," the associate said.

The dress was perfect for Jazz. She looked stunning.

"Cherise, I'll put these aside for you, but look around some more," Kaitlin advised.

"I'm perfectly happy with what we've found already," she responded. "I guess Elle and the rest of my bridesmaids will need to come see the dress we picked out."

Kaitlin laughed. "I showed them a picture of it and they all loved the dress."

"Great," Cherise said. "Now we just need to find a dress for my mother."

Kaitlin held up a beautiful ivory gown with gold sequins and said, "I put this one aside because I was thinking the color would really look good on you, Aunt Arlene."

Jazz located another dress. "This one is nice too," she told Arlene. "You should try them both."

Their selections made, Cherise took her family to a nearby restaurant for lunch.

"You are probably the easiest bride I've ever worked with," Kaitlin said as she scanned her menu.

"Once we decided on the theme, I guess the rest of it became easy." Cherise laid down her menu. "I've been planning my wedding since I was ten years old. Only thing that's changed is the theme."

Jazz took a long sip of her water. "I'm thrilled for you, Cherise, but right now the

169

only thing I want to talk about is what we're going to order."

Everyone burst into laughter.

CHAPTER 15

Cherise handed Bridgett a towel as the teenager stepped out of the pool. "You did great today. Anne tells me that you're a quick learner."

Wiping off with the fluffy towel, Bridgett smiled. "I'm okay. She's just a good teacher. I never thought I'd learn to swim."

Checking her watch, Cherise groaned. She needed to be on her way to pick up Steven's aunt. They were having lunch together. Cherise had made the gesture so that it would give them a chance to get to know one another.

"I have to leave, but I'll see you before you go home, Bridgett."

"Okay, Miss Ransom."

Cherise rushed to her car and made her way to Steven's parents' home. "I'm so sorry I'm late."

"Honey, you're fine," Eula Mae assured her.

They arrived at the seafood restaurant twenty-five minutes later.

"My goodness, Cherise," Eula Mae said. "You didn't have to bring me to such a fancy place. You could've just taken me to Kentucky Fried Chicken and I would've been just as happy."

She nodded toward the menu Eula Mae was holding. "Please order whatever you'd like. Just think of it as a fun fancy treat."

Eula Mae frowned. "Cherise, honey, I think they gave us the wrong menus. These prices certainly can't be lunch specials."

Cherise bit her lip to keep from smiling. "It's okay," she assured her. "Don't worry about the price — just order whatever you want."

Eula Mae peered over at the table next to them. Lowering her voice, she whispered, "You're very sweet for bringing me here, but I should pitch in. I can't let you pay this much for a little bit of nothing."

Cherise shook her head. "It's my treat, and I'm not taking no for an answer."

Eula wasn't convinced. "You're sure?"

Nodding, she added, "Besides, this is my way of thanking you."

Clearly confused, Eula Mae asked, "Thanking me for what?"

"Just for being so warm and friendly

toward me," Cherise said. "I want you to know that I really appreciate that."

"Well, that's because I believe my Stevie's a very lucky man. He's found himself a wonderful woman to marry, and I'm so happy for you both."

Cherise broke into a smile. "I can't tell you how thrilled I am that you feel this way about me, Mrs. Stewart. The way Steven talked about you — well, I was a little intimidated."

"I've always wanted Steven to be happy, that's all. He's a very special man, and there are some women out there who would eat him alive." Eula Mae gave a small laugh. "I guess I've been real protective of him, and if I smelled a rat I sure told him so. I think it used to get on Steven's nerves though, 'cause he soon stopped bringing them around to meet me."

"I'm sure he knew you were only looking out for him."

"Well, now he has you . . ." Eula Mae peered closer at Cherise. "I'm sorry for staring at you, but you seem kind of familiar to me."

"Really?"

"Yeah," Eula Mae said. "Maybe we passed one another or something before you left Phoenix, because I've been out of the

173

country for a long time." She seemed to be searching for an elusive memory.

Cherise took a sip of water. "Well, you know what they say, everybody has a twin running around somewhere."

Eula Mae nodded. "I suppose you're right."

The waiter took their orders.

"Steven tells me you work with kids. How do you like it?"

"Mrs. Stewart, I love it," Cherise gushed. "I love those children like my own."

"Now, dear, we're almost family," Eula Mae responded. "You call me Aunt Eula Mae just like Steven does. And I insist."

"Yes, ma'am." Cherise was secretly pleased that everything seemed to be going well. Steven's aunt was a very charming lady.

While they waited for their food to arrive, Cherise asked questions about Ghana and Africa in general. They didn't have to wait long.

When the waiter walked away, Eula Mae rolled her eyes. "That man is getting on my nerve with all his slow moving. Maybe he should just go on and retire. He's way too old to be working here."

Cherise bit back her laughter as she sliced off a piece of fish.

"At least the food was ready within a reasonable amount of time," Eula Mae was saying.

Cherise waited for her to sample her food. "How is it?"

"It's good. Mmm, it's very good."

"I'm glad you like it. I hope you're enjoying yourself." Cherise had to admit she was having a good time.

Eula Mae nodded. "I am, dear. I'm really having a good time with you. Next time, though, it'll be my treat."

Cherise wasn't sure there would be a next time, but she nodded anyway. For now, she was grateful that lunch had gone as well as it had.

Humming, Cherise sat at her desk finishing up her initial assessment on a new client who had arrived earlier that afternoon.

Footsteps echoed in the hallway, slowing down near her office.

Steven stuck his head inside the doorway.

Cherise leaned back into her chair smiling, then said, "Hey, baby. I wasn't expecting to see you today." She never tired of looking at the man she was going to marry.

"Hello, sweetness," Steven responded. He walked into the office and sat down in the empty chair facing her. "So how's your day going?"

Cherise loved the deep, rich sound of his voice. "It was good before, but much better now that you're here. Why don't you ask me what you really want to know?"

She knew exactly why Steven had come to her office. A tiny part of her felt irritated, but she forced it out of her mind.

"Okay," he said, not bothering to try and deny it. "How did lunch go with my aunt?"

Cherise broke into a smile. "I think it went fine. Babe, your aunt is such a nice lady. I really like her."

Steven gave her a knowing grin. "See, I told you that the two of you would get along. And you were so worried about meeting her."

She chuckled. "Okay, so you were right. Satisfied?"

Steven rose to his feet, then moved to shut the door. "Not until you come over here and give me a kiss."

Smiling at him, she responded, "Gladly."

The phone rang, interrupting them.

She sighed. "I guess I should get that."

"Just let it ring."

"You know I can't do that."

Picking up the phone, she stated, "Cherise Ransom speaking."

When she finished her call, Cherise pushed out of her chair and walked from around her desk.

She wrapped her arms around him and said, "Now for that kiss."

He kissed her gently on the lips, before saying, "I'd better head back to my office. I didn't realize it was getting so late. I have a meeting scheduled in an hour."

Cherise walked him out, then returned to her office.

Ransom Winters arrived a few minutes later.

"Hey, cousin," she said.

He smiled. "Thanks for making time to see me, Cherise. This center is nice. I like it."

"I'll give you a tour if you'd like."

He nodded.

Cherise showed him around the facility as they discussed his structured day program.

"I think what you're doing here for these girls is incredible," Ransom told her.

"Thank you," she responded. "Now tell me more about what you have in mind."

They returned to her office to talk.

". . . Instead of sitting at home, they can be here working on missing homework or class assignments."

"I'm going to bring in my director. I think

Maxie should hear this," Cherise told Ransom.

Eula Mae opened the front door and stepped aside to let Steven and Cherise enter the house. "Well, isn't this a surprise, Cherise. I didn't know you were coming with Stevie."

She wrapped her arms around the petite woman. "Hi, Aunt Eula. I'm sorry I haven't called you back, but it's been crazy for me at work."

Eula Mae waved away Cherise's words with a slight wave of her hand. "It's fine. I'm sure you're very busy, with your new promotion and all."

"Well, when Steven mentioned he was coming by tonight for a visit, I wanted to come, too. I hope you don't mind?"

"Shucks, no," Eula Mae said. "I'm glad you came. Stevie's parents are away at a conference, so it's just me and Jerome here at the house. I was just about to fix dinner — you go on over there and sit with Stevie. I hope you two will stay for dinner."

Smiling, Cherise nodded. "On one condition — you let me help you cook."

Eula Mae smiled in return. "Sure. Just follow me."

Pulling her close, Steven whispered, "I

never thought I could love you any more than I do now."

"I hope that you'll always remember this feeling when we are at odds with each other."

In the kitchen, Eula Mae said, "I'm thrilled Stevie has a woman like you in his life. You're good for him."

"He's good for me, Aunt Eula Mae," Cherise responded. "No one has ever made me feel so loved — outside of my family, that is."

"He is right about one thing," Eula Mae said, pulling the chicken out of the oven. "There's something very special about you. I'm not normally the type of person to just take to people, but I've grown to care for you, Cherise. My daughter didn't live, but if she had, I'd want her to be like you."

"Thank you for saying that," Cherise said softly.

"I mean it, sugar."

Dinner was ready twenty minutes later.

Jerome joined them just as they sat down at the table. He had been on a conference call.

When Steven blessed the food, Cherise sent up a quick prayer of her own. She was so thankful to be surrounded by so many loving people. After all the sadness in her youth, Cherise was grateful for the life she had now.

They discussed wedding plans while they ate.

"Well, I think a Mediterranean-themed wedding is nice," Eula Mae said. "I've never been to one like that, so I'm excited."

Steven reached over and grabbed Cherise's hand. "We are, too," he responded. "There was a time I wondered if I'd ever get married, but now I realize that I was just waiting on this beautiful woman to come into my life."

They left his parents' house shortly after nine.

Back at home, Cherise and Steven decided to end the evening in the Jacuzzi. "This water feels so good," Steven announced.

Staring up into the moonlit night, she agreed, "Mmm, you're right. I love evenings like this." She loved being out here like this, letting the moon kiss her body while the stars twinkled like golden eyes looking down upon her.

The brilliant moonlight played on Steven's muscular form, giving him a resemblance to an African god, Cherise thought, feeling her body tremble as though afire even in the depths of the cool water.

Treading water, Steven moved closer to

her. The silken feel of the liquid surrounding them cast an erotic spell about the pair.

Staring up into the sky, Cherise stated, "I think I can see my star. Look . . . it — it's so beautiful." When she looked over at him, she found him watching her, a grin plastered on his face.

"Why are you staring at me like that?"

"You're beautiful."

"Steven, you always say the right things to me at the right time." She swam closer to him, giggling.

"Do you think your neighbors have any idea what we're about to do in the pool?"

Grinning, she shrugged. "I don't think so. The patio is enclosed — they would practically have to sit on their roof to see anything that goes on in here." He reached out to untie the strings of her top.

With his help, she was soon completely naked, and so was he.

Tracing the perfectly shaped star on her shoulder, he murmured, "You know I really love your birthmark. It's very sexy."

Cherise laughed. "Really?"

"I think so. That's what prompted me to buy you a star." He stared into her eyes. "I love you so much."

"I know I've told you this before, but I really mean it, Steven. You are my reason for being. All the hurt I've experienced in my life doesn't even come close to the happiness I've known with you these last few months."

Dipping his head downward, Steven kissed her. "All I want is to make you happy. I've never known a woman like you. I'm so proud that you allowed me into your life." He placed her hand to his bare chest. "Can you feel my heart beating?"

Cherise nodded.

"Honey, it beats for you and you only."

She pulled him close to her. "Steven, I want you. I need you to make love to me. Right now," she pleaded softly. "Love me . . ."

CHAPTER 16

Instead of going to Riverside for the Ransom clan dinner on Sunday, Steven and Cherise decided to drive to Santa Monica and walk along the pier. They had just spent Memorial Day with them, so they decided to be selfish with their time.

"This is a nice way to spend a Sunday night," Cherise murmured. "Walking along the pier beneath the stars and enjoying the smell of the ocean."

"I'm enjoying this myself." Wrapping both arms around her, Steven said in a low voice, "All day long, I thought about doing this. Just holding you in my arms with nothing but the ocean in front of us. That great expanse of water going on and on. My love for you is like that."

Cherise smiled in her happiness. "You are such a romantic, Steven. That's one of the things I love about you."

His gaze met hers. "You deserve to be

happy, baby. I'm going to spend my life making you happy."

"I plan to do the same for you. I've never felt as loved as I have with you. I wish there were more men like you."

"I had good role models. I grew up watching my father spoil my mother. They have been married all these years and they still act like newlyweds. Then there's Uncle Jerome and Aunt Eula Mae. I've never seen any two people who seem so in love."

"They are a very loving couple," Cherise acknowledged. "I've noticed the way your father watches your mother. He gets this little lusty glint in his eyes." She burst into laughter. "And they're so kissy-kissy."

Steven joined in the laughter. "So are we."

"I know but . . ."

"But what? You think just because they're in their fifties, the passion has gone from their marriage? Well, it hasn't."

Her arms folded across her chest, she asked, "And just how do you know this?"

"Because I popped over there one day and they were . . . er, busy."

Her eyes grew wide. "Really? Oh my God, what did you do?"

"What could I do? I left as quietly and as quickly as I could."

"Wow."

"What? You think it's weird or something that they still make love?"

"No. I think it's wonderful. In fact, it gives me hope. Hopefully, you take after your father."

Steven kissed her. "You don't have to worry about us, sweetheart. As long as I'm able to breathe, I'll always want you."

She pinched him playfully. "You'd better."

Steven pulled his jacket together. "It's getting a little chilly. Let's head back to the car."

As they walked, Cherise clutched his hand. "I'm really glad you and my aunt are getting along."

She chuckled. "Yeah, I guess it makes things easier for you."

"She's always been there for me, Cherise. And the one time she needed me, I wasn't there."

"What are you talking about?" Cherise asked.

His expression suddenly changed to one of hatred. "Some gangbangers broke into her house and attacked her one night. They were living in Phoenix at the time."

Cherise started to tremble. A wave of dizziness swept through her. "H-how long ago did this happen?"

"I think it's been ten years now."

She pulled away and suddenly stopped walking.

Without looking at him, she said, "Steven, you sound so angry, so filled with hate." Cherise had never seem him this way.

He nodded. "When it comes to that, I am. They nearly killed her. She was hit in the head with a bat."

She turned away from him, fighting back her tears and filled with a strong sense of dread. Cherise searched her memory, focused on an incident that had happened ten years ago.

Was it possible? Could it be?

If so, then she and Steven would never have a future together.

A sob tumbled out of her mouth and Cherise took off running off the pier and down the sandy beach toward the water.

She could hear Steven calling her, running behind her. Crying hysterically, she sank to her knees in the sand.

He caught up with her. "Honey, what's going on with you?"

"I . . . oh, God, S-Steven . . ." She couldn't bring herself to continue. "I feel so complete when you're next to me. I've waited all my life for someone like you. You and your heart of gold. I don't know what I'd do if I ever lost you." Cherise wiped at her tears. "But

186

the truth is that I d-don't deserve you."

Laying her head on his chest, she started to cry again.

"Hey, all my life I've waited for someone like you, baby," Steven assured her. "We're going to be fine. I wish you wouldn't get yourself so upset." He lifted her chin with his hand. "I love you — you, Cherise. We're going to spend the rest of our lives together."

"But there are some things that you don't know about me —"

"I know everything I need to know about you. You have a good heart. You're honest and generous to a fault."

She stiffened.

"I need to tell you something," she began.

Steven shook his head. "Honey, whatever happened in the past is just that — the past. All we need to do is look toward our future together as man and wife."

Cherise sniffed. "But will you always love me even when I mess up?"

He kissed her forehead. "I'll never stop loving you, no matter what. That's my promise to you, Cherise."

She prayed he was telling the truth.

Cherise did not sleep a wink that night.

Ten years ago, she went along with Tina,

Joyce and their boyfriends to a house in Phoenix with the intent of breaking in. Cherise didn't really want to go, but Tina had told her that this was a test to see if she really belonged in their clique.

They broke into what they had assumed was an empty house. But once they were inside, they encountered a pregnant woman wielding a baseball bat. She swung out at them, striking Tina's boyfriend.

He managed to take the bat from her and hit her with it, knocking her unconscious.

Panicked, they ran off, but Cherise tried to check to see if the woman was breathing. At one point, the woman opened her eyes and grabbed for her shirt, ripping it, but then she passed out.

Cherise called 9-1-1 before running from the house. She went home and packed up a backpack, emptied out her piggy bank and her mother's wallet, crept out and headed straight to the bus station, where she purchased a ticket to Riverside, California.

Maybe it's not the same person, Cherise kept telling herself. She never did get a clear view of the woman because the house had been dark.

She had just buried the past for good, and now it was back in the form of Steven's Aunt Eula Mae.

■ ■ ■ ■

Steven had been out of town on business for the past week but was returning home today. She'd missed him terribly but was glad to have some time for herself.

She spent some time at the library, reading through old newspaper articles dating ten years back. Cherise didn't bother searching on her computer at home because sometimes Steven used it, and she didn't want him to find out that she'd been looking into what happened.

It would bring on too many questions.

A chill ran down her spine when she found a small article about Eula Mae and the burglary. There were no suspects, the article said.

Cherise's eyes filled with tears and ran down her cheeks. She quickly wiped them away.

"I'm so sorry," she whispered. "I'm going to do everything I can to make this up to you, Eula Mae. I promise."

Rebecca and Eula Mae invited Cherise to join them for lunch, but she gently turned them down, citing a heavy caseload.

She felt too guilty to even face Eula Mae right now.

I never meant for anyone to get hurt, she thought. *I don't know why I let Tina and Joyce talk me into going with them that night. I can't go back and change anything, but please don't let her or Steven find out. I will lose them both forever.*

She went home to relax and gather her thoughts before Steven arrived. She didn't want him to see that she was troubled about anything.

He arrived shortly after six.

"I'm so glad you're back. I missed you." Cherise threw her arms around Steven seconds after he walked through her front door.

She took him by the hand and led him into the bedroom. "How was your trip?"

"It was fine," Steven responded. "I'm just glad to be home."

"That's all?" Sensing something was wrong by his tone, she quickly scanned his face. "You look tired."

He nodded. "I am."

"Why don't I run you a nice hot bath?" Cherise suggested.

"That sounds good," he responded. "I was thinking about going over to my parents' house after I rest for a few minutes. You going with me?"

"Not this time, baby. I've got a lot of work to do."

"Aunt Eula Mae told me that you've been really busy."

Cherise gave a slight nod. "It's been crazy at the center," she told him. "I'm going to go run that bath for you."

She needed to get away from him before he figured out that something was going on with her. Steven had an uncanny knack for being able to read her expressions.

Steven came down and had dinner with her, then left to visit his family. He came back to her house a couple of hours later.

"Everyone told me to tell you hello."

Cherise smiled.

He sat down beside her and asked, "Honey, is everything okay?"

She nodded without looking in his direction. Cherise felt horrible about the secret she was carrying, but there was no way she could ever tell Steven. He would never forgive her.

"Are you sure?"

"Uh-huh," she said.

Rubbing his hand across his mouth, Steven closed his eyes.

Finally, he spoke. "Cherise, I hope that you know that you can trust me enough to be completely honest. I thought we had something special between us. I at least thought you trusted me."

"I do trust you. Steven, I'm okay. Look, there's nothing going on," Cherise snapped. "I'm just tired."

His arms spread expansively. "Hey, I haven't done anything except try to find out if you're okay or if you have a problem."

She watched him as he rose to his feet. Steven was hurt, and that only served to make her feel worse. "Honey —"

"Cherise, I'm going downstairs to make myself a sandwich."

He walked out of the room before she could utter a response.

"I'm sorry for snapping at you," Cherise said when Steven returned. "Look, I don't want to fight with you. You just got back from being gone a week. We should not be arguing."

His gaze met hers. "You're right. We shouldn't be, and the thing is that I'm not sure why we are fighting." Steven bit into his sandwich.

"I had a bad day at work and I've got all this casework to catch up on," Cherise told him. "I'm sorry for taking it out on you."

He offered the other half to her, but she refused it.

"I really missed you," Cherise said. "I met

with the caterer and finalized the menu for the wedding."

"You give them the deposit?"

She nodded. "And I put down the deposit on the flowers, too. Mr. Rogers is a sweetheart."

"We've known him for a long time," Steven said before finishing his sandwich. He got up and padded barefoot to the bathroom to brush his teeth.

When he returned, Steven kissed her. "No more talking or working on case files."

Cherise smiled. "What do you have in mind?"

He bent to touch her sweet, tempting lips once more. As he kissed her, the heat generated from his body, bringing a powerful reaction from Cherise.

"Make love to me, Steven," she pleaded. "I need to be close to you."

CHAPTER 17

"What's got you in such a happy mood?" Steven asked her the next morning over breakfast.

Cherise flashed him a grin and said, "I was thinking about last night and how beautiful it was being with you. We're really good together, but it's not just about the sex." Her eyes met his intense gaze. "Steven, I have so much to be thankful for."

Sitting down beside her, Steven smiled. "I'm just glad you're happy.

"You're not hungry?" he asked, pointing to her plate.

Cherise patted him lovingly on the back, and said, "While you're eating, I'm going to go up and take my shower. Are you coming up after you're done?"

Chewing, Steven nodded.

Cherise hummed as she made her way up the stairs.

While she showered, she reflected upon

her upcoming wedding to Steven, her favorite pastime of late.

She wouldn't be able to fully relax until she and Steven actually exchanged vows.

Later on, Cherise met Elle for a day of pampering.

"Well, it sounds like you and Steven's aunt are getting along."

"We are," Cherise confirmed. "She's really nice."

Elle studied her cousin's face. "What's up, Cherise? You don't sound that happy about it."

She gave her a sideline glance. "Oh, I'm thrilled about it. I want nothing more than to get along with Steven's family."

"But?" Elle prompted.

Cherise needed to unburden herself and she knew that she could trust Elle, so she said, "There's something I need to tell you, but I'll do it when we get back to my house."

"Sure. Okay," Elle murmured.

Three hours later, they sat down on the sofa in Cherise's den.

"What's wrong?" Elle asked. "You look like you're afraid of something."

"I am," Cherise confirmed. She inhaled deeply and exhaled slowly before adding, "I've never told anyone about this and I'm begging you to keep this just between us.

You can't tell the clan or your husband."

Elle looked worried. "Okay, what's going on, Cherise?"

"I need to tell you something — it happened a long time ago, but it's haunted me forever."

"Sweetie, just tell me."

Cherise's eyes filled with tears. "Ten years ago, I made a big mistake. A mistake that hurt someone."

"Is that why you came to live with us?" Elle asked. "Why you ran away from home? I always knew that there was something that was bothering you."

She nodded.

"There were these really cool girls at school and I wanted desperately to be friends with them. I know that sounds stupid to you —"

Elle shook her head. "I know what it feels like to want to belong."

"They allowed me to hang with them at a cost," Cherise said. "I started stealing from my mom just to give them money. But that wasn't enough for them — they wanted me to prove my loyalty."

Elle frowned. "In what way?"

"They were into shoplifting, stealing from houses . . ."

"What happened?" Elle inquired.

Cherise wiped her eyes with her tissue. "I went with them to this house. It was supposed to be empty."

"There was someone there," Elle said.

She nodded. "She was pregnant, Elle. She just came out of nowhere, it seemed, and she was swinging this bat. One of the guys with us took it from her and hit her hard. I thought he'd cracked her skull."

A look of complete horror washed over Elle's expression. "Oh my Lord . . ."

"They thought she was dead, so they took off, but I couldn't just leave her like that. I tried to wake her and she opened her eyes for a minute. She grabbed my shirt and she was holding on so tight that it ripped. I was so scared. I called 9-1-1. Then I came out here."

"Do you know what ever happened to her?"

Cherise nodded. "She survived, thank goodness."

Elle wrapped her arms around her. "Sweetie, I'm so sorry you've had to carry this burden for so long. Why didn't you tell mama or your father? You could've talked to any of us — you know how much we all love you."

"I was ashamed, Elle. I didn't know what any of you would think of me, and I didn't want to lose you all."

"You tried to help her, Cherise. You did try to make it right."

"The thing is, I've seen her again. She happens to be Steven's aunt."

"The one . . ."

Cherise nodded. "It is truly a small world. After all these years of trying to move on, I come face to face with my past."

"But you had no idea before that it was her?"

"It was so dark that night, and of course she's older now."

"So then she doesn't know that it was you that was there that night?"

"No, and Elle, she actually likes me. We get along so well and Steven — he adores her. I just don't know what to do."

"I think you should tell Steven the truth. The two of you can decide whether or not to tell his aunt. Cherise, if you don't deal with this, it will haunt you for the rest of your life."

"You didn't see how angry he got when he was telling me what happened to Eula Mae. Steven will never forgive me."

"He loves you, Cherise," Elle countered. "He will forgive you."

"I guess you must think that I'm a horrible person."

Elle hugged her. "I know you, Cherise. You are a sweetheart and I love you, cousin. Yes, you exercised bad judgment, but we all have one time or another. I do have a better understanding of why you're working at the center, and I applaud you. Trust me, sweetie. If Steven is the man that I think he is, he'll forgive you."

Rising to her feet, Elle said, "I hate to leave you like this, but I have to run get my babies. Call me later if you need to talk. Don't worry, I'm not going to say anything about this conversation. You can tell them when you're ready."

"Thank you, Elle, so much for not judging me. I love you."

"I love you, too, sweetie."

She walked her to the door.

Elle was wrong, Cherise decided after her cousin drove away.

There was no way she could ever tell Steven about that night. He would never understand. She remembered how he'd reacted when he told her what happened to Eula Mae.

Her secret would have to follow her to the grave.

Cherise, her mother and sister were on their way to meet Steven at his parents' house to discuss their wedding ceremony.

Cherise was all bubbly and seemed happy, but became more subdued when his aunt joined them at the dining room table. She seemed nervous around Eula Mae, and Steven couldn't help but wonder why.

She caught him staring at her and smiled. He smiled back, searching her face once more.

Steven realized that what he saw in her eyes was fear. But what was she afraid of?

Cherise turned to face her mother. "Mama, come here. I want you to meet Steven's aunt and uncle. They just moved back to the states from Ghana."

"Really?" Arlene asked in an easy tone. "I've always dreamed of traveling to Africa."

"You should go when you can. It's a beautiful country." Eula Mae's expression grew sad. "However, it's one that's often marred with ugliness."

Arlene nodded. "I suppose we can say the same about our country, too."

Eula Mae nodded. "You're right about that. But I'll tell you this, I'm glad to be home. Home with my family." She glanced over at Cherise and said, "I'm glad my Stevie has found himself a real nice girl. Cherise is a sweetheart."

Pleased by the compliment, Arlene said,

"Thank you for saying so."

Cherise wore a smile, but it wasn't her normal smile. This one looked like it was forced, Steven thought silently.

She had been acting strangely for the past couple of weeks. There were moments when she was super emotional, then other times she was moody and didn't want to talk.

He could no longer deny it. There was definitely something going on with her.

Arlene sidled up beside Cherise as she stood looking at Rebecca's latest piece of art. "Honey, I couldn't help but notice that you seem mighty uncomfortable with Steven's aunt. Is something going on between the two of you?" She whispered.

Cherise forced herself to appear surprised at her mother's statement. "Nothing's going on," she said, feigning ignorance of any reason she would have.

Her mother was not fooled in the least. Pulling her into the living room, she stated, "Cherise Yvonne Ransom, I know you. Now come clean. What is it?"

Grabbing Arlene by the hand, she led her to a corner of the room. "Mama, we'll talk when we get home," she whispered. "I can't discuss this here."

Arlene nodded.

They returned to the dining room.

"You okay?" Steven asked her.

Cherise nodded, then said, "Why wouldn't I be? We're planning our wedding."

He didn't look convinced, but let the matter drop, much to her relief.

She was thrilled when Eula Mae and Jerome decided to go out for ice cream. Cherise and her family would be long gone by the time they returned.

Steven walked her to the car.

"I know there's something weighing on you, honey. Are you getting nervous about the wedding?"

"No, it's nothing like that," Cherise answered. "I'm looking forward to the wedding."

Steven planted a kiss on her lips. "I'll call you later."

"I love you, don't you ever forget that," Cherise blurted.

She got in her car and drove away, wondering how much longer she could keep her secret.

Eula Mae seemed clueless, while Cherise was eaten up with guilt.

As soon as they walked into the house, Arlene asked, "What's going on between you and Eula Mae?"

Cherise paced back and forth. "Mama, I

need to tell you the real reason I left Phoenix."

She sat down beside Arlene and spilled the secret that she'd been carrying for so long. "It's her, Mama, and I have to tell you, I'm so scared she's going to recognize me one day."

"Did she get that good of a look at you that night?"

Shrugging, Cherise replied, "I don't think so, but I'm not sure. She came to for a minute or so." She shifted uneasily, then sighed and said in a grudging tone, "I wish this wasn't happening." Her shoulders stiffened and her hands curled into fists.

"Stay calm, baby," Arlene said. "Don't go asking for trouble. She seems to be fond of you. I don't think you have anything to worry about."

She hesitated before she replied. "I wish I could be sure, Mama. Everything was so perfect . . . and then she moved back here."

"Cherise, I know you probably don't want to hear this right now, but I'm gonna say it anyway. I really think you should go on and tell Steven about that night. That man loves you and I know he'll understand. I just know it."

Cherise's eyes widened, "Steven may love me, but I really don't think he'll feel the same way knowing that I'm partly responsible for what happened to his favorite aunt. *His other mother.*"

"You made a mistake, Cherise and you were only fifteen years old. Hon, I wish you could've come to me that night and told me what happened."

"I was afraid you wouldn't love me anymore," Cherise confessed.

"I will never stop loving you. You're my daughter." Arlene reached over and took Cherise by the hand. "But a secret like this needs to come from you. It's less explosive that way."

"Mom, I can't tell Steven. I just can't. I know that he loves me, but he loves his aunt, too."

"Maybe you're just worrying too much," Arlene suggested. "If you don't forgive yourself for that night he's gonna know something's wrong. I still think that you should be the one to tell Steven."

Cherise shook her head no. "I can't do it. I don't want to lose him, Mom. If Steven finds out what I did he will leave me, because he wouldn't want to hurt his aunt." She put her hands to her face. "I just wish that night had never happened."

Chapter 18

Cherise sat on the edge of Steven's king-size bed, watching him pack a bag for his business trip. "I wish I could go with you, honey."

"I wish you could, too, but you'd be bored to death. I'm going to be in meetings all day. Besides, you can't just up and leave your mother like that. This is the last trip I have to make before our wedding."

"You're right. I'm just really going to miss you," she murmured huskily. Out of respect for her mother, Steven had ceased spending the night at her house, and Cherise didn't stay over with him either.

"Hmm, maybe you *should* join me in New York."

Cherise eyed her nails. It was time for a manicure, she thought, and made a mental note to call tomorrow for an appointment. "I considered flying up on Friday night, after work, but I have to be fitted for my wedding gown on Saturday morning."

Zipping up the garment bag, Steven stated, "Well, I'll be home on Sunday. I have a meeting that morning, but I should be home by noon."

Cherise wagged her finger at him. "You behave while you're gone."

Grinning, he nodded. "Always, baby. There's no other woman out there for me."

"You just remember that, Steven Chambers Jr."

He pushed her down on the bed.

Steven's mouth came down on hers in a hot, explosive kiss.

Cherise swore she'd die long before he got around to appeasing the maddening desires he had roused from her. Her body felt like clay in a sculptor's hands as he mapped the contours of her trembling flesh. He covered her body with intimate kisses, causing her to crave more, to beg for all he could offer.

They were like two ravenous creatures that could not get enough of each other, could not bear for the splendorous moment to end, and yet frantic to abate the tormenting needs that consumed them.

Afterward, Cherise whispered, "How am I supposed to go home looking like this?"

"Just pull your hair back into a ponytail."

She sat up in bed, hugging her knees. "I had curls earlier."

"You really think your mother doesn't know what we've been doing?" Steven asked with a chuckle.

"I don't have to throw it in her face."

"You're going to be my wife in another month, so it'll be okay."

"You don't have to face my mother," Cherise said as she climbed out of bed. She walked into the bathroom and climbed into the shower.

Steven joined her a few minutes later.

Later, Cherise walked into the house with her hair in a bun. Arlene and Jazz took one look at her, then burst into laughter.

"You are so busted," Jazz told her. "You had curls for days when you left here."

Cherise felt her face flush in embarrassment. "Jazz, will you shut up!"

Arlene just shook her head. "I guess I'll pick up some cards or a game so that you and Steven will have something special to do on your wedding night."

Cherise's mouth dropped open in surprise. "Mom . . ."

"Well, y'all doing everything before the wedding, so what's left?"

"Yeah," Jazz intoned. "What's left?"

Laughing, Cherise picked up a pillow

from the sofa and tossed it at her sister.

Cherise grabbed the towel off her bed and wiped her face.

She was breathing heavily because of her aerobic workout and had to take several deep breaths before she could answer her ringing phone. "Hello."

"Hi, Cherise, dear. You sound as if you had to run for the phone. Did I catch you at a bad time?"

"No, I just finished working out. How are you?" Cherise held her breath while she waited for Eula Mae to state her reason for calling.

"I'm fine. I'm calling to see what you're doing tomorrow. I know Steven's out of town, so I thought I'd invite you and your mother to go to church with me, and afterward, you and Arlene can have dinner with us."

There was a pregnant pause before Cherise responded. She sat down on the edge of her bed. "Thank you for the invitation, Aunt Eula Mae, but we're going out to Riverside to see my aunt. Maybe we can plan to do it next Sunday."

"Sure, that'll be fine. Let's plan on that, okay?"

Rolling her eyes, Cherise murmured, "I'm

putting it on my calendar now."

She hung up the phone and dropped back down to the floor, preparing to resume her workout, when the phone rang again.

This time it was Steven.

"Honey, I won't be back until eight tomorrow night."

Cherise didn't hide her disappointment. "What?"

"Something came up and my boss requested another meeting," Steven explained. "I need to be here."

"I understand," she responded. "But I'm not at all happy about it."

"I know you're going out to Riverside, so don't worry about picking me up tomorrow night. I'll take a shuttle home. Enjoy yourself and tell everyone I said hello."

"I can still pick you up."

"Honey, you can't just eat and run. Stay and have a good time with your family."

After she hung up with Steven, Cherise decided to go upstairs and take a long, hot bath. She really missed him and couldn't wait for him to come home.

She ended up spending the evening with Ivy and her daughters. Ivy was having an emotional moment after having a fight with her ex-husband, so Cherise went over to cheer her up.

"Have you talked to Michael since the wedding?"

Ivy shook her head. "Not really."

"Why don't you reach out to him?" Cherise suggested.

"I can't do that," Ivy responded. "I cheated on him in college, and when he forced me to choose — I chose Charles."

"Michael doesn't strike me as they type of man who holds a grudge."

"He has my number," Ivy stated. "He could've called me. He hasn't, so I don't think he's interested."

"Ivy, call the man," Cherise urged. "He may not know that you're interested in him."

"It's too late for us. I had my chance and I blew it."

Cherise embraced Ivy. "Well, then, I guess I need to buy you a huge teddy bear or something, so that you'll have something to keep you warm at night."

"You know you are wrong, don't you?" Ivy hit her on the arm with a throw pillow.

Sunday evening, Cherise came home expecting to find the house empty, but instead she found Steven stretched out on the couch sleeping.

Cherise shrieked with pleasure, waking him.

He stood up and embraced her.

"I'm so glad to see you," Cherise told him. "I thought you weren't going to be home for another couple of hours. You said your plane wouldn't get in until eight."

Sitting up, he grinned. "I lied. I wanted to surprise you."

"Did my mother know about this?" Cherise asked. "Is that why she wanted to stay with Aunt Amanda?"

He nodded.

She gave him a light jab in the arm. "If I weren't so happy to see you, I'd be mad at you."

Steven threw back his head, laughing. "I missed you, too."

Cherise handed him a plate that was laden with baked chicken, candied yams, corn on the cob and potato salad. "Aunt Amanda sent this for you. Eat it while it's still hot."

Standing up, he headed into the dining room with Cherise following. He asked, "How did it go? Did you have fun?"

"I had a wonderful time with my family. They are always special." Cherise laughed. "Nyle and his wife are having a baby."

"Really?" He pointed to the other plate she carried. "What's that?"

She nodded and sat down across from him. "Oh, this is a piece of three-layer chocolate cake. Ivy made it."

Steven raised an eyebrow. "I hope that's for me." He dove into the potato salad, eating with relish.

"It is," Cherise confirmed with a laugh. "She knows how much you like it."

"Oh, Aunt Eula Mae wants you to go shopping with her next Saturday. She still hasn't found a dress."

Cherise's smile disappeared. "I thought she and your mother went shopping already." She pushed away from the table.

"Where are you going?" Steven asked, frowning.

"To get you something to drink," she responded. "I don't want you to end up choking from the way you're shoving that food down your throat."

Steven gave an embarrassed laugh. "I guess I was starving."

"Why didn't you make yourself a sandwich or something?"

"I knew you'd be bringing home a plate from your aunt's house."

Cherise shook her head in disbelief. "Men . . ."

Steven stood in the doorway, his hands

folded across his chest. "Woman, what's taking you so long? You don't want to be late for your own bridal shower."

Cherise sucked her teeth before replying, "Honey, I'm hurrying as fast as I can. I'm pretty sure they won't start without me."

She donned a black pants suit she'd purchased just for the occasion. Eyeing herself in the mirror, she knew she looked great.

In truth, Cherise felt really good. She walked across the hall to the guest room where her mother was staying.

Knocking on the door, Cherise called out, "Mama, are you ready? We're leaving in a few minutes." Her mother had flown in the night before, and they'd been up late talking.

"I'm just about," Arlene responded. "Come in and help me with this zipper, will you?"

Opening the door, Cherise eased into the room. She eyed the burgundy dress Arlene wore. "Wow, Mama. You look so pretty."

"Why, thank you, baby. You look pretty snazzy yourself."

Cherise wrapped her arms around Arlene. "I can't tell you enough how glad I am that you're here. This year has been my happiest in a very long time."

"I can tell you're feeling better about Eula Mae."

She glanced over her shoulder and then nodded. "I've finally put the past to rest. I'm only looking forward to the future."

Steven rapped on the open door. "You beautiful ladies ready to leave?"

"We're ready," they chorused.

The trio headed downstairs.

Steven opened the front door and stepped into the chilly breeze. Thirty minutes later, they pulled into the parking lot of La Maison, the restaurant owned by Kaitlin's husband, Matt.

After helping Arlene out of the car, he assisted Cherise.

"You all made it," Kaitlin said when they entered the private dining room. "I was just about to call to find out if something happened."

"It was your cousin's fault," Steven said.

He was rewarded with a punch in the arm.

The room had been transformed into a Mediterranean paradise. The brilliant blue colors of Greece were draped throughout the room, while brightly colored sunflowers and wine-colored candles represented Italy and Spain.

"It looks nice, doesn't it?" Rebecca said as she and Eula Mae joined them. Steven spoke to his mom and aunt before giving Cherise a kiss goodbye. He and Matt were meeting up with the Ransom men for a game of basketball.

Guests were arriving, so Cherise went to greet them.

Shower guests were served an antipasto platter representing the rich flavors of the Mediterranean. Buffet tables were laden with various hot entrées representing the different countries.

Hostesses served them while they talked and laughed.

Elle walked over and gave Cherise a hug. "How's it going?" she whispered.

"Fine," she whispered back. "I think I can finally move on."

"Did you . . ."

Cherise shook her head. "I decided to take it to my grave." For the moment, she felt safe and happy.

The turbulent emotions she'd felt earlier had dissipated. In a sense she felt reborn, felt as if she had been given another chance. Cherise looked forward to her wedding day. It would be the finest moment of her life.

Every now and then she would catch Eula Mae watching her, but Cherise made sure to keep her expression blank. She didn't want to make the woman suspicious.

After they finished eating, they settled down to play the traditional bridal-shower games.

Cherise had never laughed so hard. It pleased her that everyone seemed to be having a good time.

Elle handed the winner of bridal bingo a prize, then announced, "Okay, that's the last game. It's now time for Cherise to open her gifts."

"Jazz, dear, where on earth did you find that skimpy nightie?" Rebecca asked after Cherise opened her gift from her sister. "It leaves nothing to the imagination."

"Mrs. Chambers, that's the way it's supposed to be."

Cherise broke into embarrassed laughter. "I don't know, Jazz. This is a bit much." She held up the matching panties with one finger. "Crouchless panties? *I don't think so.*"

"Aw, don't be trying to act like a prude around your soon-to-be mother-in-law." Kaitlin said. "There was a time . . ."

She glanced over at her mother, who said, "Me, too."

Gasps of surprise went around the room while Amanda gave her daughter an innocent smile.

"Don't be embarrassed, Cherise," Eula Mae stated. "You do whatever you have to do to keep Steven in your bed and not someone else's. Have a pole installed if you have to."

"Eula Mae!" Rebecca tried to look shocked.

"Come on now, Rebecca. Now, I know you are still wearing those little sexy outfits that Steven Sr. likes . . ."

"We're not talking about me," Rebecca quickly interjected. "We're here for Cherise."

Everyone burst into another round of laughter.

Rebecca cleared her throat and handed Cherise another gift-wrapped package. "Why don't you open this one? It should be safe — it's from your mother."

Cherise winked at Arlene. "I don't know. Mama has a weird sense of humor at times." She untied the ribbon and removed the paper quickly. "Ooh, this is exquisite." She fingered the delicate ivory lace. "Mama, it's beautiful."

"I'm glad you like it. I thought it would be perfect for your wedding night."

Cherise crossed the room and planted a kiss on her mother's cheek. "Thank you."

"Open mine next," Eula Mae pleaded.

Cherise gasped. "Oh my goodness! *Pearls?*"

"Yes," Eula Mae responded. "I bought those pearls for my own wedding day, and I'd like for you to wear them on yours. I know this is a lingerie shower, but I also figured you could wear these to bed, too, and nothing else."

"Mmm," the women in the room chorused.

"They're beautiful, Aunt Eula Mae. I promise I'll give them back right after the wedding . . ." Cherise grinned. "I mean after the wedding night."

"Oh, you don't have to return them," she told Cherise. "I'm giving them to you. They would have gone to my daughter, had she lived . . . I want you to have them because you've become like a daughter to me."

Cherise's bottom lip trembled.

Guilt filled her to the core, making her feel sick inside. Not knowing what else to do, she handed the pearls back to Eula Mae. "I-I'm sorry, but I can't t-take these."

Fighting her tears, she rose to her feet and ran out of the room.

"Cherise, please tell me what happened back there?" Elle asked. "What is going on with you?"

"I can't take it, Elle. *I just can't take it.*" Cherise burst into fresh tears.

"What?" Elle embraced her. "What is it?"

"I can't take her being so nice to me like this. Not after what happened."

Cherise ran her hand across her face to wipe away her tears. "I feel like such a hypocrite. I really thought I could get past this until she handed me those pearls. This guilt's tearing me apart. I don't know if I can take much more of this."

Elle gave her cousin a hug. "I'm so sorry, Cherise."

Cherise hugged her back, and then just stared off in space. "I'm so afraid she's going to remember one day. I really like her and I don't want . . ." She couldn't finish the thought. It was just too painful.

"Maybe she didn't get a good look at any of you. You said it was dark." Elle tried to reassure her. "You've got to pull yourself together and stop tripping like this or she's going to start suspecting something."

She met Elle's worried gaze. "I know."

The front door opened and Eula Mae Stewart was standing there.

"Will someone please tell what is going on?"

Elle and Cherise exchanged nervous glances.

Eula Mae repeated her question.

Swallowing hard, Cherise rushed to Eula

Mae. "I'm so sorry for running out like that."

She glanced back at Elle. "This wedding has got me so emotional and when you said what you said —"

Eula Mae cut her off. "Shh, baby. I understand. This is an emotional time for a bride. Child, every little thing made me cry when Jerome and I were engaged."

Cherise smiled, feeling a little more relaxed. "I feel like such an idiot."

"You shouldn't feel that way. We all understand." Elle took her by the hand. "Why don't we return so that you can finished opening your gifts? I'm sure Mama and everyone is getting worried."

Eula Mae hugged her tightly. "I meant what I said earlier, and I won't take no for an answer. I want you to have those pearls."

"Thank you," Cherise murmured. Deep down she felt like a horrible hypocrite, but she managed to make it through her shower.

That evening Cherise took solace on her porch, still troubled by the gift from Eula Mae.

She abandoned her seat on the wooden rocking chair and walked to the railing, staring out with unfocused eyes.

Eula Mae had gifted her with a beautiful pearl necklace that was meant for her daughter. Weariness sliced through her, regret and guilt sapping her energy.

She yearned for Steven's comfort and his strength. She didn't really know what to do with the sentimental gift. How could she wear it, knowing what she'd done to Eula Mae?

Emotionally drained and her eyes heavy with fatigue, she stepped away from the window and made her way upstairs. Completely dressed, Cherise lay down on top of the comforter, turning on her side. She was too confused and exhausted to make a decision she might regret later.

CHAPTER 19

"Thank you, Cherise, and congratulations on your upcoming wedding. Here is your gown."

"You've outdone yourself, Garnette," Cherise said. "This gown is so beautiful."

She reached over to hug the elderly seamstress standing nearby. "I don't know what I would've done if you hadn't been here to help me."

"I just love making the dresses perfect for brides to wear. It's such a joyous occasion. I enjoy being a part of that."

Cherise carried the garment bag that contained her wedding dress in both hands, while Elle carried the boxes containing her slip and other accessories.

At home, Elle helped Cherise unload the car. "I can't wait for your wedding day. This is so exciting, Cherise."

Giggling, she nodded. "I know, Elle. I can't believe that Steven and I will actually be husband and wife in two weeks. It still seems so hard to believe." She headed to the kitchen. "I need to change clothes. I'm dying to put on something comfortable."

"I need to go pick up my children, so I'll give you a call later," Elle promised.

She left.

Cherise changed into a tank top and a pair of shorts. She was about to go into the kitchen to fix a salad when she heard a car outside.

Peeking out the window, she whispered, "It's Aunt Eula Mae. What does she want?"

"Hello, Aunt Eula Mae." Cherise hugged her. "How are you?"

"I'm fine. I stopped by to see if you —" She stopped short, catching sight of the bag on the sofa.

"Is that your wedding gown?"

"Yes, ma'am. Would you like to see it?"

"If you don't mind," Eula Mae responded.

Cherise unzipped the bag and gently pulled out the gown.

Eula Mae's eyes were bright with unshed tears. "Cherise, this dress is gorgeous. You are going to look so beautiful."

Cherise ran a nervous hand down the dress. "Do you think Steven will like it?"

"Of course he will," Eula Mae said. "Honey, he's going to love it."

She helped Cherise put away the gown.

Cherise barely noticed that the strap of her shirt had slid downward. "You know that Steven —"

A low, menacing scream ripped from Eula Mae and hung in the air for a long moment.

Jerking around, Cherise asked, *"What is it?"*

Her frightened gaze met Eula Mae's and she saw such a look of savage fury that she retreated a step, putting a bit more distance between them.

Eula Mae's eyes could have been forged in ice. Gone was any trace of her earlier friendliness; gone were the signs of acceptance. In their place was a look of pure hatred.

Dread curdled her stomach and she wished desperately that she were anywhere but alone in that room with Eula Mae.

Resigned to her fate, she acknowledged that it had been inevitable from the beginning that the truth would come out. Cherise had held stupidly to the hope that she would never have to tell Steven what happened that night.

"It's you," Eula Mae hissed. "You and those no-good friends of yours broke into my house."

■ ■ ■ ■

"Please let me explain," Cherise began in a low, tormented voice. "I can explain everything."

Eula Mae was muttering to herself. "That birthmark . . . shaped like a star. I remember *you.* How could you . . ." She shook her head. Her mouth curled into an accusing sneer as she slowly advanced upon Cherise. *"Didn't you?"*

Wrapped in a cocoon of anguish, Cherise nodded, unable to speak, her eyes bright with unshed tears. She held the top of her dress clutched tightly in her hands.

Seething with mounting rage, Eula slapped her as hard as she could. "How dare you come into my life and try to steal from me again. You won't have Steven. I won't let you take him from me."

Sobbing hard, Cherise wiped furiously at her tears. The stinging she felt on her cheek did not compare to the pain in her heart at the moment. She had to find a way to make Eula Mae understand. "P-Please let me e-explain. I'm sorry. I'm so sorry. It was an accident."

"So you and your friends accidentally broke into my house. You meant to break into another house. Is that it?" She raised her hand as if to strike again.

Retreating, Cherise covered her face with her hands. "I never wanted to be there. I knew it was wrong. They ran off and left, but I called 9-1-1 to get you some help. *You've got to believe me.*"

"I don't have to do nothing," Eula Mae shouted. "But I will tell you this. You better end this farce with my nephew."

Cherise wiped at the tears streaming down her face. "What are you talking about?"

"I know why you never said anything to me, but does Steven know the truth about you?"

Wincing, Cherise shook her head. "I wanted to tell him, but I couldn't," she said. "I just couldn't."

"I'm sure you couldn't," Eula Mae mocked. "And I bet I know why. Because he would've up and left you. If it hadn't been for me seeing your birthmark you would've gotten away . . ." She glared at Cherise. "You gotta call off this marriage —"

Her voice breaking, Cherise said, "I love Steven. I can't . . . I can't do this. He would be so devastated."

"Humph!" Eula Mae scoffed contemptuously. "You can and you will. Do you hear me? I want you out of Steven's life. You're not good enough for him."

"Please, Mrs. Stewart, please don't do this . . ." Cherise responded with an anguished plea.

"I don't want to hear nothing you got to say." Eula Mae's expression was bitter. "Steven will listen to whatever I tell him. He always has."

She left Cherise standing in the middle of the room, trembling.

Her body shook so badly that Cherise had to grip the banister as she climbed the stairs.

Staring at herself in the mirror, Cherise broke into fresh tears.

She and Steven would never be man and wife. The mere thought of not growing old with him made her feel lightheaded.

Cherise surveyed the bedroom where she and Steven had spent so many wonderful nights. She loved him so much, and leaving him like this was tearing her apart. "I can't just walk out of your life without saying something. I can't."

She sat down and wrote a note.

Putting it in her purse, she grabbed her car keys.

Reaching the door, Cherise leaned against the wall, hugging herself, squeezing her eyes, attempting in vain to stop the hurt.

She deserved this, she told herself. Her brain knew that she never would've told Steven about that night. Instead, she would have continued to pretend it never happened.

She drove to his house and slipped it into the mailbox.

He would hate her, yes. And Cherise knew she would have to find a way to live with it.

Tears filled her eyes and she walked faster to her car.

Cherise got inside and drove across town as quickly as she could. She didn't stop until she was at her aunt's house in Riverside. She couldn't get out right away because she was crying so hard.

Emotions spent, Cherise sought to contain herself. She wiped away her tears with the back of her hands.

"Oh, Steven. I'm so sorry. I l-love you so much," she whispered. "I hope you'll forgive me one day."

Steven stood in the middle of his bedroom, complete disbelief written all over his face. Cherise had called off the wedding and didn't want to see him anymore.

She was gone.

But why?

He had known from the moment his

mother handed him the envelope that it contained bad news.

Reading the contents a second time, Steven flung the letter across the room. "What in hell is going on with you, Cherise?"

His expression grew hard and resentful. Putting his hands to his face, he growled. How could she leave him like this? And then she leaves a note with a flimsy excuse at best. He deserved much better than this.

He was going to find Cherise and get some answers.

Grabbing his keys and jacket, Steven rushed downstairs and left the house.

He jumped into his car and drove over to Cherise's house, hoping to talk some sense into her.

Steven tried her cell phone and was only mildly surprised when he received no answer. Well, he wasn't going to let her just drop a bomb on him like that and take off without an explanation. She owed him that much.

Steven took the exit off the freeway that led to her street.

Arlene was the only one home when he arrived.

"She's not here," she told him. "Steven, she just needs some time to think."

"I need to talk to her."

"Just give her a couple of days," Arlene suggested.

"This doesn't make any sense, so what's going on with her?" Steven asked. "Where is she? Please tell me."

Arlene met his heavy-lidded gaze. "Do you truly love my daughter?"

"I do," Steven confirmed. "I love her with my very being."

"I'm going to ask you that same question again — after you talk to her. Whenever she was troubled about something, she always went to Amanda. I don't know why, but that's where she found her peace."

He called Amanda Ransom's house but was told that Cherise wasn't there.

Following his instincts, Steven drove to Elle's house.

When he arrived, Elle looked completely surprised to see him. "Steven, what are you doing here?"

"I came here to speak to Cherise. Elle, I know that she's here and I really need to talk to her."

Folding her hands across her waist, Elle announced, "Cherise doesn't want to talk to you right now, Steven. She loves you but she's got some things to sort through and she needs time. Can you give her that?"

"Elle, what's going on? None of this is making any sense to me. Was she unhappy?" His voice was low, almost begging.

Elle shook her head sadly. "No, she wasn't unhappy. Just give her some time and I'm sure she'll come to you and explain everything, Steven." She lowered her voice and put her hands on his arms. "Trust me when I tell you this. She loves you with her whole heart, but she needs you to do this for her right now."

Despondency washed over him. Only an innate sense of pride enabled Steven to hold back his tears. "She's my life, Elle."

"And you're hers," she responded. "Steven, if you love Cherise, and I know that you do, just give her time to sort things out."

"But she's called off the wedding —"

"Cherise will come to you when she's ready."

His mouth opened, but no words came out. He stared at Elle, feeling rejected and helpless.

Sighing in resignation, Steven turned and headed to the door. "Elle, tell her that I love her — that I always will."

Standing at the window, Cherise watched him drive away, her heart breaking all over again.

CHAPTER 20

Elle closed the front door behind her, locking it.

Cherise turned from the window to face her cousin. "I hated seeing him like that."

"What do you expect? He's heartbroken, Cherise."

Breathless seconds passed while Elle's words reverberated through her brain. She squeezed her eyes shut against a rush of tears. "So am I. Elle, I never wanted it to be like this." Her voice broke miserably. "I don't know how I'm going to make it without Steven in my life. He was the best part of me."

"He feels the same way about you." Elle took Cherise by the hand and led her to the couch. "I saw something in Steven I've never seen before. He's in agony over your leaving. That should tell you something, Cherise. That man loves you beyond definition. Tell him about that night. Tell him

232

everything."

She stiffened momentarily. "I can't. I don't want him to hate me any more than he already does."

Cherise couldn't breathe, so she rushed over to the window, opening it with trembling hands. She inhaled deep, calming drafts of the night air.

Elle came behind her. "Steven doesn't hate you. *You hate you.* Cherise, you've never forgiven yourself for what happened to Mrs. Stewart. And you've got to do that. Even if she never forgives you."

"I don't think Steven could forgive me either."

"You haven't given him the chance."

"I'm scared."

"Look where you are now, Cherise," Elle pointed out. "You've called off your wedding. What more do you have to lose by telling him the truth?"

She paused as if waiting on a response from Cherise. When none was forthcoming, she asked, "Will you at least think about what I've said?"

"There's nothing to think about, Elle. It's over between Steven and me."

Although she wore a disapproving frown, Elle offered no further comment.

Alone in the guest room, Cherise couldn't

concentrate, her thoughts clinging to Steven and the agony he must be going through. But he wasn't the only one suffering. All she had left were the raw sores of her aching heart.

Desperately wishing there had been another way, Cherise sighed sadly.

Dreams are often hard to separate from reality, Cherise discovered as she was slowly awakened by the alarm clock. Before she opened her eyes to the new day, Cherise stretched on the firm mattress, remembering the way Steven's strong hands felt around her. She missed waking up beside him. She missed his laughter.

She missed everything about him.

"Steven." His name escaped her lips before she could stop it.

Turning on her side, Cherise brushed away a lone tear. The full impact of her situation hit her. She and Steven would never have a future together.

As she sat on the side of the bed, Cherise reasoned that the pain would stop one day.

Almost as tired as she had been before going to bed, she forced herself not to think about her restless night as she went to the closet and began to select what she would wear today.

Check Out Receipt

Hayner PLD-Downtown Library (HYNP-ZED)
618-462-0677
www.haynerlibrary.org

Monday, June 10, 2024 6:00:11 PM
EVERAGE, JO-JENA L

Item: 0003005343388
Title: YOU AND I
Call no.: OTF
Due: 6/24/2024

Total items: 1

You just saved $20.00 by using your library. You
 have saved $687.53 this past year and $5,658.78
 since you began using the library!

Access free eBooks, audiobooks, digital magazine
s, and stream unlimited movies and TV shows with
 your Hayner Library card! Ask for more informat
ion at the Circulation Desk.

9-30-25 ✓
9:15
new Dr Testoserat

9-26-25
MÉsadan
8C 9.30

With her mind turned to survival, Cherise readied for work. She promised herself that she would not allow her personal heartbreak to interfere with the job she had to do.

Dressed, she headed downstairs and into the kitchen. Elle greeted her.

"Morning," Cherise said dryly. "I hope you slept better than I did."

"Not really. Briana had a slight fever and was up most of the night."

Cherise blew on her coffee lightly. "Really? How is she feeling now?"

"I think she's doing better. She's upstairs sleeping in her daddy's arms like nothing's wrong. I'm going into the office for a few hours, but Brennen's working from home today." She glanced up at Cherise. "Have you decided what you're going to do?"

Cherise shook her head. "I don't know what to do."

"Yes, you do. You tell Steven the truth."

Checking her watch, Cherise decided it was time for her to head to the center. "I'm going to keep thinking about it. I want to be honest with Steven — I just don't want him to hate me afterward."

"He won't, Cherise. He loves you too much."

"I want to believe that, Elle. I really do."

"You need to give Steven a chance."

As she drove to work, Cherise considered Elle's words. Maybe she was right. She wondered how Steven would feel knowing that Eula Mae had forced her out of his life.

Maxie strolled past her office and then backtracked. "I didn't expect to see you today. I thought you were off until the wedding. What are you doing here?"

Cherise didn't respond.

Maxie adjusted her glasses and peered down at her. "Is something wrong?"

"Steven and I are not getting married," she said quietly.

"You're kidding, right?"

"No," Cherise said. "We . . . we broke up, Maxie."

Completely at a loss for words, she dropped down in a nearby chair. "Cherise, I . . . I'm so sorry. I really don't know what to say. This is the last thing I ever expected to hear."

Apparently sensing that nothing more would be forthcoming about the breakup, Maxie cleared her throat. "Well, I'd better get back to my office. I've got a busy day ahead." She paused at the door. "Cherise, if you need anything . . ."

"Thanks, Maxie." When she was finally alone, Cherise put her hands to her face and closed her eyes.

A lone tear escaped from beneath her eyelids and rolled down her cheek. She felt bereft and desolate.

No matter how much it hurts, I have to move on with my life, she told herself.

Focusing on her work, Cherise worked through the morning and most of the afternoon.

Maxie stood in her doorway. "Have you left your office at all today?"

"No, I was so busy —"

"Cherise, dear heart. Please go to lunch. You need to get out of this office. Get some fresh air."

Putting her pen down, she leaned back in her chair. Cherise nodded in agreement. "You're right." She rose to her feet. "I'm going to get a bite to eat. I won't be gone long."

Cherise knew what she needed to do.

Steven drew in his breath when he spotted Cherise standing in the hallway. She was still very beautiful but he noticed that she looked tired. He cleared his throat and called her name. "Cherise . . ."

Composed, her head held high, she asked, "Can we talk?"

He nodded. "I was just about to head out for lunch."

They drove to a park near his office.

He got out and walked to the passenger side, opening the door for her.

"Cherise, why did you call off our wedding? Honey, please tell me what's going on. When two people love one another, the only way to work things out is to talk about them."

In response she only shook her head, refusing to look at him. "This isn't easy for me, Steven. I know that you deserve an answer."

Gently, he grasped her by the shoulders and guided her to a nearby picnic table. When she still refused to look at him or let him embrace her, Steven took her hands, holding on to them when she tried to pull away.

"Tell me what I did wrong, Cherise. Whatever I did, I'm sorry." He placed her hand to his heart. "My heart beats for you, sweetheart. *Only you.*"

Cherise couldn't look him in the eyes.

Bewildered, his patience began to ebb. "I need you to explain this to me, Cherise. What in hell happened to us?"

Her head jerked up. "Steven, please." She pulled her hand away from his heart. "You didn't do anything wrong. I messed up."

Cherise gathered her courage, because it

was time to get this over with.

Steven studied her face. Something was troubling her deeply. His fingers itched to run his hands up and down her body, to massage her tense shoulders.

Cherise was biting her lip. Suddenly, she drew in a quick breath.

Gathering courage, Steven thought. But for what?

They sat in stoic silence.

Steven spoke first. "I think I deserve to know why you called off the wedding."

Her gaze met his and her expression became intense — so intense that he felt a moment's discomfort before her scrutiny.

Finally Cherise responded. "You're right, Steven. You do deserve an explanation. I'm going to tell you everything."

He heard the trepidation in her voice. "I'm listening."

A slight movement brought his attention to her hands. She was twisting them nervously. "Ten years ago, I was running around with a bad crowd. We did some things I'm not proud of . . ." her voice faltered.

"Go on," Steven prompted. He could see a tightening in her body. "I know all that." Foreboding surrounded him, chilling the air. "Is there more?"

Cherise swallowed hard, then cleared her throat. "Yes . . . well, one night we broke into a house. It was dark. There weren't any lights on or anything. The house was supposed to be empty."

His back stiffened. "What happened?"

"When we got inside, we found a woman inside." She was watching his face carefully.

Those words made his mouth fall open, and his heart thudded to a stop. It seemed to him that his brain refused to function, except to fill his head with a sickening, dizzying roar.

Shaking his head, Steven tried several times to breathe normally. He resisted the urge to spring to his feet and pace. "Noo —"

Cherise turned her wide eyes on the man she loved, who looked as though he had been struck a horrifying blow. The very agony on his face mirrored that inside her heart. "I did what I could to help her. I called 9-1-1. She wasn't supposed to get hurt," she said at last. "No one was supposed to get hurt."

Feeling his hands tremble, Steven made fists. The words wouldn't form, but the truth hit him in the face. "You're telling me that you're partly responsible for . . ." He

240

couldn't say the words.

"For what happened to your aunt." Blinking rapidly, Cherise finished for him. Nervously, her hand gripped the edge of the picnic table.

This time Steven gave in to the impulse and rose to his feet. He just stood there, staring into space. After a while, he turned around to face her.

Cherise wanted so much to comfort him. Standing up, she closed the space between them. They faced each other, each with their own thoughts, each speculating on the thoughts of the other.

Finally anger fought through the suffocating layer of pain in Steven's heart to become anguish. "Did you know who she was in the beginning?"

Moisture blurred her vision and Cherise's hands were shaking badly. "No. It was so dark that night in the house, I didn't get a clear look at her. I didn't realize it was her until you told me what happened." She was talking entirely too fast but she couldn't pause for fear she wouldn't finish. "I was afraid she would remember one day. And she did."

"What are you talking about?"

"She recognized my birthmark." Cherise gazed at him, her wide eyes dark with pain.

"When I was trying to see if she was still breathing, she grabbed my shirt and ripped it. I didn't know that she'd seen my birthmark."

Cherise raised her face and looked at him with pure, agonized embarrassment in her eyes. She could hear the pain in his voice, and the sound of his heart breaking. "She told me that I didn't deserve you."

Tears brimmed in her eyes and she heaved a shuddering sob.

Pacing back and forth, Steven kept muttering over and over, "I don't believe this."

With a look of pure agony, he asked, "Why did you keep this from me?"

"I tried to tell you, but you kept saying that the past should stay in the past." Cherise rose to her feet. "I'm so sorry, Steven. I really am."

He moved his shoulders in a shrug of anger.

To her dismay, Steven wouldn't even look at her, keeping his back to her. "I need to get out of here. I need some time to digest all of this."

When he finally turned around, loathing issued from his eyes, from the hard set of his mouth, from his stance.

She had hurt him deeply. Cherise doubted that she could ever make it up to him. Wanting to comfort him, Cherise reached to touch him; Steven deflected her fingers, and his eyes were like ice chips. "I'm sorry, but I can't."

She opened her mouth to speak, but changed her mind. Tears streaming down her face, she whispered, "I'm so sorry, and I have regretted that night ever since. I will do anything to make this up to you."

Steven gave her a sharp look. He could not control the trembling of his body. Cherise, the love of his life, was responsible for what had happened to his aunt? He could not believe it. It had to be a mistake. But it wasn't. He'd heard it from Cherise's own lips.

Crossing his arms, Steven walked back to the car.

Cherise followed him.

They got in without saying a word to one another. As soon as they reached his office, Cherise got out of his car and walked briskly to her SUV.

Steven barely noticed when she drove out of the parking garage. He was still numb from the shock. His throat turned dry and blood pounded at his temples. His stomach clenched tight like a fist.

She still dominated his thoughts when he returned to his office. Steven slammed a

243

hand on the desk in front of him, frustrated by her betrayal. The pain he felt was real, devastating, acute. His head throbbed with it, his lungs constricted with it.

Steven's thoughts centered on his aunt. What was he going to say to her or his mother? He probably should call to check on his aunt, but he couldn't bring himself to do it just yet. He needed some time to sort the situation out himself.

CHAPTER 21

Cherise went to her bedroom and climbed into bed, curling up into the fetal position, her mind tormented.

How would she be able to begin to live without Steven and with all the pain she'd caused Eula Mae?

The next day, Cherise stayed in bed and refused to answer the phone.

Arlene couldn't get her to eat anything.

Elle came over, so Cherise assumed that either Jazz or her mother had called her. When she entered the bedroom, Cherise was sitting in the middle of the bed, hugging her knees.

She took one look at Elle, buried her face and cried. Inside, she wanted to die.

Elle eased down beside her. "I take it you told Steven everything."

Wiping her tears, Cherise nodded.

"How did it go?"

"He hates me, Elle."

"No, I don't believe that," she said. "I'm sure he's probably in shock, but he doesn't hate you."

"You didn't see his face," Cherise argued. "It had disgust written all over it." Unable to restrain herself, she broke into fresh sobs.

"Cherise, I'm going to tell you the same thing I told Steven when he came over to my house looking for you. Give him some time."

Past her closed throat, she asked, "How can he ever forgive me?"

"He will . . . because he loves you."

Cherise shook her head.

"Yes, Cherise. Steven loves you. He'll come around. I know it," Elle assured her.

"You were always the romantic, Elle. Happy endings don't always happen, you know."

"But you will have a happy ending. I can feel it, sweetie," Elle said. "You will."

"No, I won't," Cherise said sadly. "Our love disintegrated when I told Steven the truth about that night."

Elle embraced her. "I'm so sorry."

"It's not your fault," Cherise said. "I should have been honest with him from the very beginning. Maybe things would've turned out differently. Then again, his aunt would still hate me."

■ ■ ■ ■

Two days passed without another word from Steven.

Cherise began to accept that she and Steven were finished. She flew to Phoenix with her mother just to get away from Los Angeles. "I guess I need to take my house off the market. I'm going to need a place to live."

"I was hoping Steven would have called you by now," Arlene commented.

Rubbing her shoulders, Cherise shook her head. "It's over, Mama. We have to accept it."

"It doesn't have to be over, hon. You and Steven can still work this out, if you want to work it out. You two have paid out all that money on this wedding, and then the house is almost ready. You need to have another conversation with this man."

"Mama," Cherise stated flatly. "There's no way to fix this." She paused to stand in front of the huge picture window. "But you're right, we do need to talk."

Arlene had cooked a fabulous dinner, and they talked about the past while they ate.

Cherise wiped her mouth with a corner of her napkin. "Dinner was great, Mama."

"I'm glad you enjoyed it. I cooked all of your favorites."

"I know, and I appreciate it. I want you to know you're spoiling me. If you don't stop it, I'm going to expect this kind of treatment every time I come home."

Arlene chuckled.

Cherise pushed herself away from the table. She started picking up the plates and glasses. Arlene took them from her. "You don't have to do this. I'll do it."

"No, Mama. Let me do this for you," Cherise argued. "I need to keep busy, and if I'm doing something, my mind won't be on Steven or how badly I hurt."

"Well, I'll dry. It will go quicker if we clean up together."

Cherise shook her head. "Just let me take care of it, please."

"Okay, baby," Arlene said. She left her alone in the kitchen.

She and Steven were very happy together, and they clicked. Should she just give up without a fight? Cherise wondered as she washed dishes. She knew that he loved her — she didn't doubt his feelings for her. He also loved his aunt. In times of trouble, her family stuck together. It was the same for Steven. But maybe there was still a chance for them to heal and fix their relationship.

When Cherise had put the last of the dishes away, she went to her mother's room. "Mama, would you mind very much if I went back to Los Angles?"

Arlene smiled and shook her head.

"I'm going to see Steven," Cherise said. "I love him too much to just let him go like this. I'm going to talk to him and his aunt. I need to try and make things right."

"If you hurry, you can make the nine o'clock flight."

Cherise broke into a grin. "I never unpacked, so I'm ready. I'm going home to try and win my man back."

Cherise pushed her fears aside and walked into Steven's office the next day as if she didn't have a care in the world.

"Good morning, Steven." She had stopped at Starbucks on the way there and picked up a cup of his favorite coffee, which she sat down in front of him.

"Thanks for the coffee, but what are you doing here?" he asked, frowning.

"I wanted to see you," she said, taking a seat in the chair facing his desk. "There are some things that we need to discuss."

"Like what?" Steven inquired.

"How about our wedding and all of the money we've paid out in deposits? The house that we're building. You don't think any of that warrants a conversation?" she asked.

Steven got up and walked around his desk. He closed the door to the office. "I guess this couldn't wait until later."

"We are not exactly on speaking terms right now," she responded. "There's a lot of tension between us, Steven."

"I didn't put it there," he said.

Cherise kept her expression blank. She was determined not to let him get to her.

"I will buy out your share of the house," Steven announced.

She gave a slight nod.

"All of the deposits were nonrefundable, so we can't recoup them."

"I will pay you back the money you put down," Cherise offered. "As you stated earlier, it's my fault that we're not getting married."

"You don't have to do that," he said.

"I want to," Cherise told him. "Steven, I love you, and I'm not that same little girl anymore. I made a mistake."

"The mistake was not telling me as soon as you realized that my aunt was the woman you attacked."

"I didn't attack her," Cherise said, her voice rising an octave. "I tried to help her."

"Cherise, I don't want your money."

"Then what do you want?" she snapped. "To be free of me? I remember you telling me that you would love me forever."

He met her gaze straight on. "That hasn't changed. I still love you, Cherise."

"Then why can't we work this out?"

"You don't have any idea what that attack did to her, Cherise. That's why they didn't move back to Phoenix — it was too many bad memories. How could I bring you back into her life? It would be a constant reminder. She may look strong, but she's not. She's very fragile. I was young, but I remember that my aunt would suffer anxiety attacks if she had to stay in that house by herself."

Cherise's eyes filled with tears. "So there's no way for us to get past this?"

"I wish there was," he murmured.

She rose to her feet. "I guess we have nothing else to discuss, then. I'll let you get back to work."

"Goodbye, Cherise."

Steven's heart broke into a million little pieces as he watched Cherise walk out of his life. He still loved her and probably would never stop, but he couldn't hurt his aunt by bringing a constant reminder of the past back into her life.

He tried to focus on his work, but couldn't.

Steven decided to call it a day around lunchtime.

He went to his mother's house because he wanted to check on his aunt.

"Where is Aunt Eula Mae?"

"She's in her room lying down."

"How is she doing?" Steven asked. "Did she tell you what happened?"

Rebecca nodded. "How are you?"

"There's not going to be a wedding," he told his mother.

"Why not?" she asked. "Steven, you love Cherise, don't you?"

Steven hadn't expected that reaction. "Mom, you do know what Cherise did, don't you?"

"She was a child," Rebecca responded. "Eula Mae knows that."

"She was one of the people who hurt Aunt Eula Mae. As fragile as she is, I can't let Cherise into her life to constantly remind her of that night. It's not right."

How could she take sides with Cherise? She was Aunt Eula Mae's sister. She knows what happened back then, because she'd had to take care of her until Uncle Jerome arrived from Ghana.

When his aunt was feeling better, she joined him and had been there for ten years.

Steven made himself a sandwich but found that he really wasn't hungry.

The doorbell rang.

He was surprised to see Brennen standing on his porch.

Steven stepped aside to let him enter the house.

"Elle told me what happened between you and Cherise. Is there anything I can do to help?" Brennen asked.

He shook his head no. "I still love her, but we have no future together."

"The mere fact that you love her says otherwise, Steven. Love can overcome a multitude of sins. Trust me, I know."

"I had this perfect picture of her in my mind, and it's been shattered. The woman I thought she was would never have done what she did."

"Steven, did you ever take the time to get to know the real Cherise and not the one in your imagination? We all have our women on pedestals, but it's because we placed them there — they don't just jump up there. You have to get to know the whole woman — the real woman."

"So you think that I love the one in my mind?"

"What do you think, Steven? Your wedding is less than two weeks away and you and your fiancée are at odds with each other. I know that Cherise loves you and she wants to be your wife. She made a mistake when she was fifteen years old. Haven't you ever made a mistake, Steven?"

"My aunt is haunted by that night. I can't do this to her."

"So you're choosing her over Cherise?"

"I love them both, but I saw the way my aunt grieved. Losing her daughter tore her world apart. I can't have a constant reminder of that night in my life."

"Cherise is a wonderful woman, Steven, and if you don't want her, she will find a man who will love her unconditionally." Brennen got up and walked to the door. "I'll see myself out."

Chapter 22

The Ransom women showed up on Cherise's doorstep to rally around her. Seated all over the den, they dispensed advice.

"Honey, you shouldn't give up like this. Don't you cancel one thing on this wedding," Ivy advised. "I can't believe I'm actually saying this, but you fight for that man. You two love each other."

Kaitlin agreed. "If Steven wants to cancel the wedding, let *him* do it. Don't cancel a thing. Right now, he's probably not thinking clearly, but tomorrow he may feel differently."

Cherise turned around to gaze at Amanda. "What would you do?"

"I don't think I'd give up. I'd keep fighting until the very end, but I'd start with Eula Mae. She put this all in motion by threatening you, so go to her and try to talk this thing out."

"She hates me, Aunt Amanda."

She shrugged in nonchalance. "You still insist on speaking with her. Start there."

"I think Mama's right," Elle said.

Jillian and Allura agreed.

"I think someone needs to knock some sense into Steven," Regis said. "Men can be so hardheaded at times."

All of the women agreed.

"But we didn't give up on them," Regis continued. "Cherise, Laine put me through some stuff."

"Really?"

She nodded. "I'll have to share that story with you sometime. I didn't think we were going to make it."

Carrie agreed. "Ray and I have a story like that, too. We had to come to a meeting of the hearts."

Kaitlin laughed. "Well, you all know that Matt and I had serious drama."

Cherise nodded. "We all thought you were dead. I had never seen a man grieve so much. It broke my heart to see Matt back then."

"But even after that, we almost didn't get married."

"My life with Garrick has been nothing but loving and drama-free, thank the Lord," Daisi said. "No story here."

Allura raised her hand and said, "Same

here. I'm not complaining though. I like being drama-free and boring."

They laughed.

The doorbell rang.

"Are you expecting someone?" Ivy asked.

"No," Cherise responded, shaking her head.

"I'll see who it is," Jillian said. She got up and went to answer the door.

Cherise was shocked to hear Rebecca's and Eula Mae's voices.

"What are they doing here?" Elle asked in a low voice.

"I don't have a clue," Cherise responded.

"We didn't realize you would have company," Rebecca said when they entered the den, "but maybe it's good that you're all here."

"Why is that?" Amanda asked. Her tone was cool.

"Eula Mae is here to talk with Cherise, and I think that it's a good idea that we're all here."

"Why?" Eula Mae demanded. "Only Cherise needs to hear what I have to say. Although I've said all I need to say. I don't know why you brought me here, Rebecca. It's not going to change a thing."

Rebecca shook her head. "I don't agree. We have two people who love each other and they have been ripped apart. It's not right."

"I agree with that," Amanda said.

"Was it right to have my head cracked by a bunch of gangbangers?" Eula Mae uttered. "Was that right?"

Her words cut Cherise like a knife.

Jillian got up and made room for them to sit down.

"Aunt Eula . . . Miss Eula Mae, I'm . . . you will never know how sorry I am and how much I regret what happened," Cherise told her. "I don't have any excuse for what I did, but I am really truly sorry. I tried to make sure that you got help."

Eula Mae glared at her. "I know that you weren't the one who hit me, Cherise, but you were there in my house uninvited. I thank you for calling the paramedics, but they're the ones who saved my life — not you."

"I hope that one day you will be able to forgive me."

Eula Mae did not respond.

"Elle, could you do me a favor and get the pearls for Miss Eula Mae?" Cherise asked. "I was going to mail them to you, but since you're here, I can give them to you now."

"Why are you staring at me like that, Rebecca?" Eula Mae demanded. "I didn't do a thing except try and treat this girl like family. I thought the world of you, Cherise."

"She made a mistake. She was a child," Amanda interjected. "Eula Mae, I had Cherise with me from that time until she left for college. She has made great strides to be a much better person. She has agonized for years over this — I didn't know what was going on with her, but I always knew that there was something bothering her."

"None of that changes the fact that Cherise was one of the people who broke into my house that night. I was hit in the head with a bat by one of the boys with them. *They left me for dead.*"

"But Cherise called 9-1-1," Elle said. "The paramedics saved you, but so did Cherise, whether or not you want to admit it, Mrs. Stewart. If she hadn't called them, you might have died without anyone realizing for days."

"And I suppose you think she should be pardoned, then."

"I'm so sorry, Miss Eula Mae," Cherise kept saying. "I truly am."

Rebecca sent a sharp glance in her sister's direction. "I know you're angry, but how can you hurt your nephew like this?"

The room was so quiet, you could literally hear a feather drop.

Wringing her hands in resignation, Rebecca sighed heavily. "Eula Mae, it's time for you to forgive."

Her sister didn't respond.

Cherise reached out, pulling Eula Mae to her feet. "I understand why it's hard to forgive. I don't know if I'll ever forgive myself for what happened that night."

The two women embraced each other tightly.

Eula Mae took Cherise's face in her hands. "You and Steven deserve to be happy. I'm sorry I tried to destroy that. If I'd ruined Steven's happiness I don't know that I could forgive myself."

"Mrs. Stewart, can we please start over? Would you please give me a chance to earn your forgiveness?"

They just stood there holding onto each other.

"Cherise, why are you still here?" Ivy asked after Eula Mae and Rebecca left the house. "You need to go to Steven."

"You might want to shower and do something with that hair first," Jillian suggested.

Laughing, she nodded.

Cherise sent up a prayer of thanks as she showered and dressed to see Steven. It occurred to her that maybe she should give him a call before popping over there.

She picked up the phone and dialed his cell.

It went straight to voice mail.

She called his office and was told that he was away.

Cherise was getting frustrated. She tried his cell once more, and again it went to voice mail.

"He's not . . ." her voice died when she saw Steven standing in the middle of her den. Cherise glanced around, but there was no sign of her cousins or Aunt Amanda.

"They all left," Steven told her. "In a hurry. I tried to explain that they didn't need to leave, but they insisted for some reason."

She smiled. "They wanted to give us some time alone."

Cherise sat down and so did Steven, only he chose the overstuffed chair instead of the sofa where she was sitting.

"They really didn't have to leave," he said.

She could tell that he was still very distant with her, so she said, "Steven, I understand totally why you're upset with me and I don't blame you. I did a terrible thing and then on top of that, I kept it a secret from you. I've apologized and I'll do it again and again

261

until you believe me. I love you and I want to make this work between us."

"I don't hate you," he told her. "You just . . . you took me by surprise. It's like the woman I thought I knew so well, I didn't know at all."

"Steven, have you ever done anything that you're so ashamed of?"

"Yes."

"Well, what happened that night when we broke into your aunt's house is my shame. I was so ashamed, I ran away from home — I couldn't even face my mother. Your mother and your aunt came over earlier. Miss Eula and I talked and we've made peace. Why can't you and I do the same?"

Steven looked surprised. "They were over here?"

She nodded. "You didn't know?" Cherise had assumed that was why he was there to see her. "If you had no idea that they came by, then why are you here?"

"I brought some of the stuff you left over at my house and I came by to pick up my things."

Cherise stiffened in shock. "Oh."

"I'm glad you and my aunt made peace, but I still can't get over the fact that you never once tried to come to me after you discovered she was the one you hurt."

"You keep acting like I picked up the bat and swung on her," Cherise said, not bothering to hide the anger in her voice. "I didn't do it, Steven. I didn't tell you because I was afraid of losing you. Deep down, I really wanted to tell you. I did, but then you spouted off hatred for the people who hurt your aunt. Do you actually think I would come to you after that?"

"I expected you to be honest, Cherise."

"How do you feel about me now?" she asked quietly.

"I don't know. Right now, I just don't know. I didn't come here to hurt you, Cherise."

She refused to look at him. "I know."

"Cherise . . ."

Holding up her hand to stop him from saying more, she ran out of the room.

CHAPTER 23

Steven felt like kicking himself. He hadn't meant to upset Cherise like this. He had come over because he wanted to see her and to pick up his things, but mostly he just wanted to look at her because he missed her.

Hearing footsteps, he turned around.

Cherise stood in the middle of the room, biting her bottom lip. When he moved toward her, she looked ready to bolt.

"Cherise, I'm sorry if I upset you. It was not my intent."

She shrugged. "You can't help the way you feel."

"I care about you, Cherise. Please don't forget that."

"Don't," she said. "I really don't want to hear it. I asked you just a few minutes ago how you felt about me and you didn't know. Let's just leave it at that. Just get your stuff and leave."

"I'm in an awkward position and I'm not sure what to do, Cherise."

"Why don't you go talk to your aunt," she told him. "I think that should clear up some things for you."

Cherise seemed deep in thought. Steven watched her for a moment before asking, "What are you thinking about?"

"About how much I'm going to miss you. I thought you were the best thing to ever happen to me and now . . . you're just a jerk."

"Excuse me?" he asked with a frown. "What did you just say?"

"You're a jerk," Cherise repeated. "How dare you try to diminish what we've shared because of a childhood mistake?"

She was getting angrier by the minute. "You have not always been the person you are now. You have flaws — big ones, Steven — but you don't see me bolting out of your life. I've told you over and over to take me off that pedestal of perfection because it wasn't me, but you wouldn't listen. Now you're disappointed and so you want nothing more to do with me. Go on and leave, because right now I can't stand the sight of you."

He was floored by her words.

Cherise was hurt and angry, so she was

striking out at him. He wanted to comfort her. Hell, he wanted to make love to her.

Steven loved her with all his heart, but he couldn't bring himself to tell her so. From the pained expression on her face, it looked to Steven as if she needed to hear him declare his love.

He couldn't. Steven couldn't, because every time he thought about loving Cherise, he felt a constant thread of guilt weaving itself through his body.

"Please hurry up and leave," she told him. "I want you out of here."

"Cherise, wait . . ."

"Lock the door behind you," Cherise said. "I can't do this with you right now."

Wiping her tears from her face, Cherise stared out into the dark, starless night. How would she be able to survive without him? She loved him with her whole soul.

Elle called her later that evening.

"How are things going?" she asked.

"They aren't," Cherise responded with a sob in her throat. "Steven doesn't know how he feels about me."

"Did he tell you that?"

"Yeah. He hasn't spoken to his aunt yet, so he doesn't know the whole story. The thing is, he should trust me or know me well enough to see the truth." Cherise wiped away a tear. "I don't need a man who will instantly believe the worst about me. I deserve much better than that."

Elle agreed. "Would you like me to contact everyone and cancel the wedding?"

"N-Not yet," she murmured. "Let me think about it. I'll probably just do it myself . . ."

"I'm so sorry, cousin. I thought Steven . . . Anyway, it's his loss."

"Yeah, it is," Cherise said. "Elle, could you call everyone and please, tell them I'm fine? I really just want some time alone."

"You're sure?"

"I just need to be by myself for a few days."

"You are going to come to Riverside, right?" Elle asked. "I don't think you should be alone."

"Yes. I'll be there. Mama's already got her ticket, so she'll be here tomorrow. I'm going to have her stay with Jazz."

"I love you, cousin."

"I love you, too, Elle. Thanks."

They hung up.

Cherise curled in a fetal position, sobbing until no more tears would come. Then she got up and showered, pulled her wet hair into a ponytail and made her way downstairs, where she sat down in the den and watched television.

Steven didn't want her, but she would find a way to go on with her life.

She thought about the star he'd named for her and she blinked rapidly to keep from crying.

"I guess you weren't the one after all," she whispered.

Steven walked into his parents' house and said, "I heard you and Mom went to see Cherise."

"We did," Eula Mae said. She sounded tired and looked like she'd been crying.

"Are you okay?" Steven inquired.

She nodded. "I guess Cherise told you what we talked about."

"She just said that you two made peace. That was it."

Eula Mae looked stunned. "She didn't say anything else?"

He frowned. "No, why?" Steven couldn't figure out what else could there be. "Is there more?"

"I just thought that she . . ." Eula Mae's voice died.

"What is it?" Steven asked.

"Stevie, I need to tell you something," Eula Mae said. "I hope that you won't hate me when you find out what I've done. I never meant to hurt you."

"I could never hate you," he told her, stroking her cheek. "Aunt Eula Mae, please tell me what's going on."

"I told Cherise to call off the marriage. I told her that if she didn't, I would tell you what happened. I'm so sorry."

He nodded in understanding. "Aunt Eula Mae, I don't hate you. I could never hate you."

"I was wrong for the way that I treated Cherise and I told her so. I apologized to her. Son, she really is a lovely girl."

"Aunt Eula Mae . . ."

She turned to face him. "Steven, if you want to marry her, then you need to get over there and make things right. I'm so sorry I messed up everything for you two. If you don't get married, I don't know if I'll ever forgive myself."

"It's not your fault what happens between me and Cherise," Steven said. "I messed this up by not believing in her. I knew that she wasn't a bad person deep down, but it was just hard to fathom that she'd be a part of a group of people like the ones who hurt you."

"Your Uncle Jerome was once a Blood."

Steven's mouth dropped open in shock.

"Are you serious?"

She nodded. "He was even shot once by a rival gang member — that was enough to get him to leave that lifestyle behind. My daddy used to tell us this all the time: you are not who they say you are, even though you did what they say you did. I'd forgotten about that until now. Cherise is a good girl who was in the wrong place at the wrong time. I have a better understanding of why she works at that center. She doesn't want them to make the mistake she made."

He nodded. "She says that all the time."

"I'm sorry, Steven."

"I don't know if she'll take me back after the way that I treated her," he told Eula Mae. "I hurt her pretty bad."

"We never give up, right?"

Steven smiled at her. "Right."

When he left the house, Steven considered going to see Cherise, but the hour was late and he wasn't sure she would ever speak to him again. He decided to wait until tomorrow.

He felt like a major heel.

How could I treat the woman that I love like this? He prayed that Cherise would forgive him this time around.

CHAPTER 24

Steven pulled into the parking lot of the Darlene Sheppard Center and found an empty parking space near the front.

As soon as he entered the building, he ran into Maxie Sheppard.

She gave him a bright smile and said, "Hello, Steven. It's good seeing you again."

"You, too," he responded. "Maxie, do you have any idea where I can find Cherise?"

"She's in the pool area with some of the girls."

"Can I watch unobserved? I don't want her to know I'm here. Not yet anyway," he said.

Maxie nodded. "Sure. Just go on upstairs to the observation room."

"Thanks, Maxie."

"No problem."

Cherise was sliding down in the water until she was fully submerged. Suddenly she started kicking and yelling for help.

His initial thought was that she was drowning. Steven rushed through the double doors and jumped into the water without thinking. It occurred to him after he jumped in that she was an excellent swimmer.

"Steven, what in the world are you doing?"

"I thought . . ."

The teens in the pool were trying hard to hide their laughter.

"You were teaching them how to save someone who's drowning," he said sheepishly.

Cherise nodded, then burst into laughter. "What are you doing here?"

"I came to save you."

"Your BlackBerry is ruined," she said. "I hope you have insurance."

She assisted him out of the pool.

"I've just made a major —"

"It was very sweet," she told him. "But I hope you have some clothes in the car."

"I do." Steven studied her face, trying to read Cherise's expression, but he couldn't. She was polite but not as openly expressive as she normally was.

"You go to the restroom and change out of this stuff. Give me your keys and I'll go to your car and get your bag."

A few minutes later, Steven was in dry clothes and struggling to ignore the whispers and giggles as he and Cherise walked down to her office. She closed the door behind them.

"Now, why are you here?" she asked. "Actually, it's good that you're here. I was about to cancel everything for the wedding."

Steven met her gaze. "Cherise, I don't want a life without you. I want you in my life and in the house we bought together. I love you, Cherise. I want you to know that has never changed."

"A few days ago, you didn't know how you felt about me," Cherise responded. "Steven, I'm sorry, but no."

"I admit that I was wrong, sweetheart. I know that you were just a kid and what happened left you with an invaluable lesson. I know deep down in my heart that you don't have a mean bone in your body. Cherise, I trust you with my life."

She rose to her feet and started pacing back and forth. "I don't know about that."

"I love you, Cherise."

"Please don't do this, Steven," she pleaded. "I can't do this."

"Can I come over tonight?" he asked.

Cherise folded her arms across her chest. "For what?"

"So that we can finish this discussion," Steven replied. "I'm not going to make this easy on you. I was a fool before, but I won't make the same mistake twice."

Cherise stared out of the window with her back to him.

"Please . . ."

She turned around to face him. "We can talk, but I have to be honest with you, Steven. I'm moving on. I'm tired of living in the past."

He flashed a sexy smile. "I'll see you tonight."

Cherise was speechless.

How could Steven think that they could pick up where they left off just like that? The man had lost his mind.

She couldn't believe him.

Cherise forced Steven out of her mind until she made it home that evening. She changed into a pair of sweats and sat down to wait for him to arrive. Her stomach was a bunch of nerves.

I can't let him get to me, she vowed silently as she thought of the intimacy they'd once shared. *He's hurt me too much.*

She heard a car pull up into the driveway. *He's here.*

She opened the door to let him enter.

Steven embraced her, then released her. Cherise swore she could feel the heat of his light touch clear down to her toes, bringing back delicious memories.

When they entered the foyer of the house, Steven turned to her saying, "I love you, sweetheart, and I know that you love me, too. We are so much a part of one another that separate we're nothing. You're my better half, and I need you in my life, Cherise."

She still loved him with her whole heart. She wasn't sure she could just let him walk out of her life again. "Can you truly forgive me, Steven? Can you look past any flaws that I have and love me for me?" She asked the question quietly but firmly and waited for his answer with breathless anticipation, hoping he would say what she longed to hear.

Sitting across from her and holding her hands in his own, Steven's eyes appraised her. "There's nothing for me to forgive. I accept you and your past. I'm sorry that it took me so long to get to this place."

Cherise felt the sting of tears.

Still holding her hands within his own, Steven placed them against his broad chest. "I want you to marry me."

Looking up into his handsome face, Cherise could not speak for a few seconds. She thought she was dreaming, but as his words began to permeate every portion of her mind and soul, she stepped away from him. "Steven, you really want to marry me?"

He smiled. "I can't live without you."

Steven could not resist the sweet temptation of her lips so close to his own and for a moment his mouth slanted over hers and drank the sweetness. "Please say that you'll be my wife."

Cherise's heart swelled with happiness and she covered his face with kisses. "Yes, Steven. Yes, I'll marry you," she said.

Steven pulled her into his arms. "Baby, I've missed you so much."

"I missed you, too." She replied. "This has been nothing but torture, Steven."

"I'm sorry for everything."

"I need you to trust me, but mostly to love the real me."

"I give you my word," Steven told her. "I won't let you down this time."

Cherise took him by the hand and led him to the bedroom.

After making love, Steven watched Cherise sleep. She was in his blood.

He eased out of bed and went downstairs to place a call to Elle. He wanted to run an idea past her.

"Steven, are you sure this time?" Elle asked. "I like you a lot, but I won't let you hurt my cousin a second time." Her tone was firm and brooked no argument.

"I give you my word that I will never set out to deliberately hurt Cherise. I really do love her, Elle."

"I hope that you do."

"Elle, I want to surprise her."

"I won't say a word," she promised. "I'll call you tomorrow morning at your office."

He hung up and went back upstairs to join Cherise.

She was still sleeping, so he crept back into bed with her. Cherise stirred slightly, then snuggled up against him.

Smiling, Steven closed his eyes.

He was happier than he'd been in days.

CHAPTER 25

Cherise eyed the wedding gown hanging in the dressing room at La Maison. It was her wedding day.

"I can't believe this is really happening," Cherise whispered. She couldn't seem to stop smiling.

"Regis is going to be here shortly to do your hair," Jazz announced.

She hugged her sister. "I'm getting married today."

"I know. Honey, this is your wedding day and you've got to get moving." Jazz checked her watch. "Kaitlin and Elle are here, but Allura and Ivy are late. After Regis does your hair and makeup, she's going to curl my hair."

"Have you seen Steven?"

Jazz nodded. "He's here, so you can relax."

Her other bridesmaids arrived.

Jazz ushered them into the dressing room and rushed them into their gowns.

"Your sister is so bossy," Allura said.

Cherise laughed.

Regis styled her hair into an upswept style, weaving the satin ribbon with tiny rosebuds through her curls. After she finished with her hair, she applied makeup with a light hand to complete Cherise's wedding look.

Elle was zipping Cherise into her gown when a knock on the door caught their attention.

Cherise glanced over her shoulder and asked, "Elle, can you get that?"

"Sure." She peeked out and Cherise heard voices.

Elle turned and announced, "It's your soon to be mother-in-law and Miss Eula Mae."

They stepped inside of the room.

Rebecca embraced her. "You look beautiful."

Eula Mae agreed, and then opened her purse. "There's just one more thing you need," she said. "I want you to have these."

She placed the pearls around Cherise's neck. "If my daughter had lived, I would want her to be just like you. Steven is right. You are a very special lady."

Cherise blinked away her tears. "Miss Eula Mae, I don't deserve to wear these."

"Everybody deserves a second chance,

Cherise. When I met you, there was just something about you — we had a connection, and now I understand, or I think I do. We were connected that night when you tried to help me, and that connection never went away. God took my baby home to Him, but He sent me you. I've witnessed the way you have helped those kids at the center heal from life's hurts, and I believe you're my second chance to heal. I need to finally heal."

The two women embraced.

Jazz cleared her throat loudly and pointed to her watch.

Arlene smiled. "Why don't you ladies get lined up? Jules and I are going to escort our daughter down the aisle and get her married. I think Steven has waited long enough."

Looking over her shoulder, Eula Mae embraced her sister. "Our Stevie's a very lucky man."

Cherise shook her head. "No, I'm the lucky one."

"It's time," Elle said.

She could hear the music playing, and her father strolled into the room. He and Arlene greeted each other.

They walked down a long hall to where the larger banquet rooms were located.

Cherise slowed her steps as she glimpsed the poster-size drawings of her surrounded by some of the places they'd visited on the cruise guiding them to the room where she would take her vows. She knew that Steven had drawn all of them.

There were a couple featuring the two of them that he must have sketched from photos. All were beautiful, well-documented renditions of their time together.

Two Grecian statues stood on either side of the door.

"Oh my goodness," she whispered. "They're real people. That one just blinked." She glanced over at Kaitlin and smiled.

The doors opened, and at almost the same moment the harpist began playing.

The bridesmaids made their entrance, followed by Jazz.

With the ring bearer and flower girl walking in front of them, Cherise and her parents entered the transformed ballroom.

They escorted her down the aisle to Steven, who was waiting with tears in his eyes.

When it was time for them to say their vows, Cherise went first.

"I love you, Steven. Today is a very special day for me. Long ago, you were just a dream and a prayer. On this day, I have so much to be thankful for. Thank you for being what you are to me. With our future as bright as the promises of God, I will care for you, honor and protect you. Steven, I lay down my life for you, my friend and my love."

"Cherise, I love you, baby, and I know that this love is from God. Through all of the uncertainties and trials of the present and future, I promise to be faithful to you and love you. I promise to guide and protect you, as Christ does his Church, as long as we both shall live."

They exchanged rings and before the pastor could get the words out of his mouth, Steven captured her lips with his own.

Applause erupted around the room.

"I present to you all, Mr. and Mrs. Steven Chambers Jr."

More applause followed.

Later, Cherise walked over to Kaitlin and Matt. "You both did a fantastic job with this place," she said. "I really feel like I've been transported back to the Mediter-ranean. I can't wait to see what you've done with the reception."

"I can't take credit for any of this," Matt said. "It was my wife and Elle. They did a great job, though."

After the formal wedding photos were done, they made their way to the ballroom where the reception was being held.

The soft glow of the candles highlighted the hues of reds, blue, greens and traces of gold in the tablecloths. Each table featured edible centerpieces of cascading cheese, grapes and breadsticks on marble slabs. Marinated olives were placed in stoneware for guests to savor.

"Everything is beautiful," Amanda said when she joined them. "The ceremony was beautiful."

Cherise hugged her aunt. "Thank you."

Steven wrapped an arm around Cherise. "I hope you're pleased with everything."

"I am the happiest bride alive, honey. You did good. I had no idea you were going to hire people to be statues. I thought we were going to use columns."

"I just wanted to surprise you."

Cherise flashed him a grin. "It worked. People haven't stopped talking about them."

Their wedding dinner consisted of foods from France, Greece, Italy and Spain. Stations were positioned around the room representing each country. To add to the Mediterranean feel, gold Chiavari chairs with exotic throw pillows were placed at the head table.

After dinner, Steven had one more surprise for Cherise.

The lights were turned off. He gestured for her to look up.

"Oh my goodness," Cherise murmured. "Stars . . ."

Tiny, glittering gold stars adorned the ceiling.

She kissed him. "Thank you. Now I have a surprise for you, as well."

He gave her a sidelong glance. "You do?"

Cherise nodded. "Sit down and enjoy." She signaled Kaitlin, who whispered something to the D.J. they'd hired to work the reception.

She sat down beside her husband.

The music started and the doors opened to allow six women in colorful, flowing outfits enter.

Steven broke into a grin. "Belly dancers?"

Cherise nodded.

They watched the performance. Steven leaned over and whispered, "I would have enjoyed seeing you do a belly dance for me."

"That's my other surprise, but you'll have to wait until later," she responded.

Steven and Cherise dined and danced the evening away, surrounded by the love of family and friends.

"Are you ready to leave?" Steven asked with a hopeful gleam in his eye. They didn't leave until Saturday for their honeymoon, so they were going to lock themselves away in a hotel suite until it was time for their flight.

"I'm ready whenever you are."

They thanked everyone for coming and quickly made their escape.

"So, how's married life?" Elle asked a glowing Cherise a couple of days after she returned from her honeymoon. They met for lunch at the Cheesecake Factory in Marina del Rey.

"It's great," she replied. "Steven and I have never been happier or closer."

"I'm glad you're back. I missed you."

"What's going on with the clan?" Cherise asked. "Have I missed anything?"

"Not really," Elle responded. "But you will be glad to know that your father isn't seeing that woman anymore. However, my mama and Mr. Ragland are still spending time together."

"I'm glad my dad has come to his senses. As for Aunt Amanda, I'm happy for her."

"I'm not sure how I feel about it," Elle admitted.

"I have some news of my own," Cherise said. "Steven and I are trying to get pregnant."

Elle's mouth dropped open. "Really?

That's wonderful."

"I'm hoping we got pregnant on our honeymoon. Either way, I'm keeping my fingers crossed until it's a done deal."

Elle laughed. "It's going to happen in its own time. Just enjoy being a wife for now. When motherhood comes, then you're too tired to be a wife at times. I'm still trying to balance everything."

"I'm looking forward to having that problem."

After lunch, Cherise returned home.

She opened one of the boxes in the bedroom and started pulling stuff out. Cherise didn't stop working until it was almost time for her husband to leave the office.

She started dinner.

Steven found Cherise seated on the sofa in the family room reading. He planted a kiss on her forehead before asking, "How was your day?"

"I had lunch with Elle, then came back here and did some unpacking. Dinner should be ready in about five minutes."

They sat down to a meal of roast chicken, green beans and mashed potatoes and gravy.

"Aunt Eula Mae told me to remind you that you two have a lunch date tomorrow."

Cherise smiled. "I haven't forgotten."

"You two have really become close," he

said. "I think my mom's getting a little jealous."

She sliced off a piece of her chicken with her fork. "Oh, no. I'll call her this week and we'll do something special."

Cherise glanced up to find Steven watching her. "What's up, baby? Why are you staring at me like that?"

He caressed her with his gaze. "Are you in the mood for some baby making?"

Cherise smiled. "Definitely."

Steven pushed away from the table and stood up. He moved around the table to where she was sitting. Holding out his hand, he asked, "Then what are we waiting for?"

ABOUT THE AUTHOR

Jacquelin Thomas is an award-winning, bestselling author with more than thirty-five books in print. When she is not writing, she is busy working toward a degree in psychology. Jacquelin and her family live in North Carolina.

The employees of Thorndike Press hope you have enjoyed this Large Print book. All our Thorndike, Wheeler, and Kennebec Large Print titles are designed for easy reading, and all our books are made to last. Other Thorndike Press Large Print books are available at your library, through selected bookstores, or directly from us.

For information about titles, please call:
  (800) 223-1244

or visit our Web site at:
  http://gale.cengage.com/thorndike

To share your comments, please write:
  Publisher
  Thorndike Press
  10 Water St., Suite 310
  Waterville, ME 04901